"What, are you on some kind of world tour?"

"Of a sort."

Something that looked like envy flickered in green-as-the-sea eyes. The pretty parts of the ocean, not the deadly depths swelling all around Oyster Island.

When the diver's full lips parted, Kellan struggled not to stare.

Aside from visiting a peak or depth on every continent, Aoife had made him promise to be open to a fling somewhere along his travels. If she'd seen the man behind the counter, she'd have flagged Sir Cotton-Is-No-Match-for-My-Muscles as a prime candidate.

Sorry to disappoint, Eef.

The fling would have to be an Aussie. Completing the requisite certification dives in the unpredictable Salish Sea was going to take all of Kellan's energy.

"You want private training? Or group training and private dives? How many?"

"Too many," he said under his breath.

One eyebrow rose.

Kellan cleared his throat. "Private everything." It was worth the expense. Without the certification, he wouldn't be able to complete the rest of his sister's requests. "The certification dives, and then two a week until the end of March."

"And do you have a preference for a divemaster?"

Hours of being around Sam was asking for trouble...

"I want you."

Dear Reader,

The islands in the Salish Sea on the west coast of British Columbia and Washington are some of my favorite places in the world—wild and brash, breathtaking, enchanting. Is it any wonder it makes the perfect location for romance? Love at Hideaway Wharf is a new series set on Oyster Island, and I can't wait for you to visit! Kellan Murphy's new to the island, too. The famed Irish chef arrives needing to learn how to scuba dive to finish his late sister's bucket list. He doesn't expect to find a vacation fling, let alone a new home. But divemaster Sam Walker might be both.

Sam is reluctant to admit it, but running his ecotourism shop and keeping his family from falling apart has left him treading water. Kellan is a welcome distraction from his usual routine. Of course, Kellan's diving lessons aren't as easy as expected, as the Irishman is petrified of the open ocean. Getting in deep together means facing not only those fears, but Sam's own, too. Can exploring the coastal wilderness—both above and below the surface—give them the courage to dive into the best of adventures: love?

Keep up-to-date on Love at Hideaway Wharf and exclusive extras by visiting my website, www.laurelgreer.com, where you'll find the latest news and a link to sign up for my newsletter. I'd love to hear your thoughts on Sam and Kellan's story—come say hello on Facebook or Instagram. I'm @laurelgreerauthor on both.

Happy reading!

Laurel

Diving into Forever

LAUREL GREER

Recycling programs
for this product may
not exist in your area.

ISBN-13: 978-1-335-59419-8

Diving into Forever

Copyright © 2023 by Lindsay Macgowan

For questions and comments about the quality of this book,
please contact us at CustomerService@Harlequin.com.

Harlequin Enterprises ULC
22 Adelaide St. West, 41st Floor
Toronto, Ontario M5H 4E3, Canada
www.Harlequin.com

Printed in U.S.A.

USA TODAY bestselling author **Laurel Greer** loves writing about all the ways love can change people for the better, especially when messy families and charming small towns are involved. She lives outside of Vancouver, BC, with her law-talking husband and two daughters, and is never far from a cup of tea, a good book or the ocean—preferably all three. Find her at www.laurelgreer.com.

Books by Laurel Greer

Harlequin Special Edition

Love at Hideaway Wharf

Diving into Forever

Sutter Creek, Montana

From Exes to Expecting
A Father for Her Child
Holiday by Candlelight
Their Nine-Month Surprise
In Service of Love
Snowbound with the Sheriff
Twelve Dates of Christmas
Lights, Camera...Wedding?
What to Expect When She's Expecting

Visit the Author Profile page
at Harlequin.com for more titles.

For Erryn.
This one wouldn't have happened without you.

Chapter One

The bald eagle was bloody laughing at him.

The massive bird perched in a roost on the rock jetty protecting the hodgepodge of boats at Hideaway Wharf. Its tittering rang clear as day despite being on the far side of the web of slips and branched docks.

Hee, ha hee, ha hee ha ha.

Kellan Murphy stood on the wooden boardwalk, certain the bird's cries stood for *good luck making a holy show of yourself* in eagle-speak.

The high-pitched tone wasn't nearly fierce enough to suit a raptor with a six-foot wingspan. More closely resembled the over-the-phone giggles from the nights when his plastered sister would call him from uni to poke fun at him for always having to work weekends.

If only he could take lessons from the regal creature on how to dive into the choppy, jade-black depths of the Salish Sea, it might save him some humiliation.

Kellan took shallow breaths as he approached the row of quaint dockside businesses hugging the rugged shoreline of Oyster Island's commercial center, trying to clear the scent of salt and seaweed and creosote posts from his nose. When he could keep his distance, he loved everything the ocean promised— plump, mineral-forward oysters and mussels, perfect for creating magic on a plate. A little mignonette or a broth made from veg and langoustine shells, and he could make people moan with one bite.

Today, the only thing moaning was his pride.

He'd arrived on the ferry from the Washington mainland last night. This morning had been for getting his bearings before he tackled his purpose for coming to the tiny island.

Naturally, "bearings" involved patronizing nearly every business occupying the six pastel-painted houses that hugged the waterfront boardwalk. The connected buildings oozed seaside charm and reminded him a fair bit of Cobh, Ireland's famed row of colorful houses. Best he could tell, the ground level was for retail and the upper floors were residential, including the rental flat his sister's executor had arranged for him months ago. He'd given his credit card a workout already. After starting with caffeine from the bakery nestled under the place he'd call home all March, he'd been unable to resist popping into a gift shop for a bar of locally made rosemary soap that smelled like pure class. And then his crowning indulgence, a Dungeness crab Benedict at the snug bistro bookending the strip.

He'd avoided the dive shop on the opposite end up to this point but couldn't any longer. Time to pay the piper.

Or, quite literally, the proprietor of Otter Marine Tours.

He took a deep breath. He'd been diving in a pool. Next up—open water certification.

Zipping his brand-new waterproof jacket to the collar to fend off the stiff spring wind, he circled the end of the building. It was impossible to avoid the splashy marine-based mural that stretched two stories high. The otters dancing in the kelp forest were having a jolly time.

Somehow, he needed to harness that joy of being underwater.

He could do this. Hell, two years ago he'd climbed Kilimanjaro and had hiked the Tour de Mont Blanc with his sister. Late last year, he'd climbed Aconcagua without her.

But heights and depth were different things.

He'd promised Aoife he'd conquer both on her behalf. Three continents to go. Three different dive sites.

If she could face cancer, he could face an admittedly irrational fear.

He climbed the small flight of stairs to the porch-fronted dive shop. It took up the entirety of the main floor of the left-most house, tucked in next to the bustling bakery and below a space with a "for rent" sign in the window. A rack of souvenir T-shirts and a collection of stand-up paddleboards bracketed the front door.

If only his sister's list involved being on the *surface* of the ocean. That, Kellan could deal with.

Probably.

A sign—hand-painted script on a cedar shingle—hung on the door.

> *Not here?*
> *(1) Out on the water*
> *(2) Down on the dock*
> *(3) Late.*
> *(Likely, if Franci is working—she's really sorry.)*

"Sam" was written in block letters underneath, next to a ten-digit number. No doubt the same Sam with whom Kellan had exchanged a few emails.

He tried the knob. Not locked.

Too bad.

He entered the small shop, a waft of neoprene overwhelming him before he even crossed the welcome mat. Huh. He'd expected an ocean tang. The space, which looked like it had been a living room or parlor once upon a time, was empty of people and full of diving paraphernalia. He'd have to rent one of the suits hanging from a rack by the far wall, plus a tank and a regulator. He'd only brought his mask along. It had served him well in the Cayman Islands, the snorkeling he'd done in five feet of water behind a breakwater counting just enough to cross SEE PARROTFISH OFF CHEESEBURGER REEF off his sister's list.

Five feet of *crystal-clear* water, mind you. Nothing like the opaque abyss under the hull of the Oyster Island ferry, the waves slapping in time with his racing pulse.

After he completed the *tour du-monde* Aoife couldn't, he'd donate his mask and get back to work, having received the inheritance he doubted he'd ever feel he deserved.

Though he'd never get to Okinawa or the Whitsundays if whoever was in charge of Otter Marine Tours didn't materialize. Tardy Franci, perhaps, though why the place wouldn't be locked up in the absence of an employee, he didn't know. Seemed unwise, given the cost of the equipment hanging from racks and stacked on shelves.

"Hello?" he called out, ringing the bell on the small counter.

"Sorry!" A baritone voice rumbled from an open door on the other side of a dual-height, glass-topped sales counter. The taller half displayed a locked collection of dive knives. "Just a second."

"No hurry," Kellan said, never meaning something more in his thirty-four years of existence.

"Thanks."

The voice was masculine in that *purr at me in the morning* way Kellan had gone many months without hearing. Maybe the "Sam" of the block print and phone number and "someone sent you a letter care of my address" emails.

Steeling himself against the framed underwater images of ocean life on the wall behind the counter, he pretended the collection of knives was more fascinating than a display case stuffed with artisanal cheese.

The blades were blunt and rough-edged, nothing like the honed steel he used in the kitchen. These tools weren't made for slicing off paper-thin discs of beef or chopping liters of mirepoix. More like for disentangling a person from a tangle of kelp or netting, fifty feet below the ocean surface.

He shuddered.

Stop it. Spinning around, he searched for a distraction. A large poster of Oyster Island caught his eye, and he strode over to study it. He'd be living here for a month, after all. Made sense to get familiar with the place. Not that there was much to know—a road ringed the perimeter of the oblong island, with a few narrow tracks meandering through the forest and farm areas in the center. At least it held the promise of local ingredients to play with in the kitchen—

"Hi. Thanks for waiting." The voice curled around him from behind, closer this time.

Kellan turned. His jaw dropped a little before he managed to clamp it shut.

He'd not expected Adonis. *Or Neptune. Were those both Greek?* Oddly for a book nut, he had zero interest in ancient mythology and could never keep track. Gran would look at those arresting sea-green eyes and russet-tinged hair and immediately start jabbering about selkies, but Kellan didn't put much stock in the folk tales of his childhood, either.

The man standing behind the counter was avert-your-gaze attractive. Wide shoulders, brawny waist, thick thighs… By the look of his biceps, there was no need to worry about getting caught in kelp forests or fishing nets. He could rip them in two with his bare hands.

Oof. Focus, Murphy.

Not on the Otter Marine Tours logo on that T-shirt, gracing pecs that spoke of hauling heavy diving gear.

Mr. T-shirt's eyes narrowed. "You okay?"

"Sure and I—" Sweet Jesus, he sounded like a frog. He cleared his throat. "I'm assuming you're Sam, not Franci of front-door-apology fame?" A person could never be too careful.

"Yeah, I'm Sam. If you're looking for Franci, she is, as per usual, late." He grinned. Free, easy.

Even after Argentina and Grand Cayman, Kellan didn't know how to be those things.

"Funny business model, keeping on tardy staff." He cringed. His inner firing squad of late waitstaff couldn't help itself sometimes. "Bollocks, I—"

"She's the boss's sister. *My* sister." The sexy smile faltered. "Gets her a pass most of the time."

Kellan's heart cramped. *Sister.* Late and unpredictable. He knew that story, lived it once. Should have cut Aoife a break more often than he had. "Very sorry. Not my circus, not my monkeys."

"Don't worry about it. We run on island time here,"

the other man said, smile recovering. "What can I do you for?"

"I'm here to confirm my dive training, and to rent equipment." Hopefully that didn't betray any of the panic clawing in his belly.

"Oh! I should have placed your accent, but with your registration details, I was expecting English, not Irish. Kellan, right? How was your trip from London?"

"I came from the Caribbean, actually."

Sam whistled. "Nice."

"It was." He'd sound like a prick if he mentioned it being just another checkmark off Aoife's list, a tropical interlude at the halfway point between the three climbs and three dives.

"Before we deal with your dives, I have something for you," Sam said. "The letter I emailed you about."

"Ah, that. Sorry for the inconvenience."

"Nah. First time I got mail for a client, but it wasn't a problem."

Nothing. If only it was nothing, not his heart scrawled on more of that hospital letterhead and tucked into envelopes for him to discover as he traveled the world.

Sam dug the letter out from a drawer behind the counter and handed it over.

Kellan was going to have to wait to read this one. He wasn't in the mood to break down in the middle of a dive shop, in the company of someone he'd just met. He jammed it in his pocket. "Thanks a million."

"Right on." Sam gestured at a rack of dry suits.

"You can decide what style you want to rent. I have you in the group class starting on Wednesday."

Kellan winced. "About that—if you've any private lessons, I'd prefer them."

"Private dive prices are there." The flicker of intrigue that crossed the man's face must have been a figment of Kellan's imagination, because the voice was all lazy business. Sam pointed a work-worn finger at a menu hung on the wall next to the pictures of underwater doom. "For the divemaster and the boat attendant."

"Who's the divemaster?"

"A guy named Archer Frost, my sister or me."

"Who has the most experience?"

"Hours in the water?" The hottie ran a hand through his thick hair. "Arch, by a few. Logged a ton in Australia last summer."

"I'm going there next month," Kellan blurted.

"What, are you on some kind of world tour?"

"Of a sort."

Something that looked like envy flickered in green-as-the-sea eyes. The pretty parts of the ocean, not the deadly depths swelling all around Oyster Island.

When Sam's full lips parted, Kellan struggled not to stare. Would they taste like the individually packaged, white Lifesavers nestled in the giant mussel shell next to the mounted point-of-sale iPad?

Aside from visiting a peak or depth on every continent, Aoife had made him promise to be open to a fling somewhere along his travels. If she'd seen the man behind the counter, she'd have flagged him as a prime candidate.

Sorry to disappoint, Aoife.

The fling would have to be an Aussie. Completing the requisite certification dives in the unpredictable Salish Sea was going to take all Kellan's energy. Nothing left for faffing about in bed, even with a man as edible as the one standing in front of him, wearing a mildly confused expression.

"Do you want private testing? Or group testing and private dives? How many?"

"Too many," he said under his breath.

One eyebrow rose.

Kellan cleared his throat. "Private everything." It was worth the expense. Without the certification, he wouldn't be able to complete the rest of his sister's requests. And if he wanted to get on with honoring her and Gran by earning his own Michelin star, he needed the inheritance attached to this trip. "The certification dives, and then two a week until the end of March."

"And do you have a preference for a divemaster?"

He should really book with this Archer Frost fellow. Hours of being around Sam was asking for trouble—

"I want you." *Oops.* "I mean, to book with you."

"Let me check the schedule, see if I can switch up your registration. We're jammed this time of year." Brow furrowed, the diver tapped at the iPad screen. "I could fit you in on Tuesday and next Friday to take care of your certification. After that, Mondays and Thursdays should work for the rest of the month."

Three days of waiting for his first dive… Could be worse. There might have been room tomorrow, and then Kellan wouldn't have been able to enjoy any sort of delay.

He was quite sure the shop hours had said they were closed on Tuesdays, but maybe that was just for people popping in to browse. "If Tuesday works for you…"

"You said you 'need' to book."

Kellan nodded. The handwritten list folded in his wallet never failed to weigh him down, like he was carrying a rock instead of a hastily jotted note on a square of hospital stationery.

He pulled out his credit card. The list flew out and landed on the counter. He picked it up before Sam could get a good look at it. The starred caveats on lines eight and nine were bound to garner a cocked eyebrow. "I can prepay if you like. Just add on whatever gear I've a need of beyond a mask and snorkel."

"All in, for eight dives?" Sam named an exorbitant price.

Ouch. That would pay for a new deep fryer in the restaurant Kellan and his business partner were planning to open. But without spending this money, there would be no deep fryer at all.

He handed over his credit card, one step closer to another crossed-off line.

The bell tinkled as the door swung shut behind the intriguing out-of-towner. Sam Walker rolled the man's name around in his head.

Kellan Murphy.

Sam's newest client had a London address, a gorgeous Irish accent and a devastating smile. The kind of man that could make a person want to follow along to all of the places written on the dog-eared list that had fallen from his wallet.

He'd caught Alps—crossed off—and Japan before Kellan had squirreled it away.

Sam got started on his monthly equipment inspections but kept having to go back over all the dry suit seams every time his thoughts drifted to his newest client's lilting speech.

Soon after, Archer strolled in after his morning dive tour. His short dark hair was still damp from the water. As broad as Sam but even fitter from a hell of a workout regimen, Archer had the perpetual tan of a guy who was usually either out on a boat or putting his running blade to the test. He homed in on Sam's expression. He started stripping out of the base layer he wore under his dry suit, glaring. Six feet, two inches of solid suspicion. "What?"

"I need you to work on Tuesday."

Need. The word had fallen from Kellan Murphy's mouth with reluctant conviction, tightening against Sam's skin like a too-small wet suit. It had flashed in his gray eyes, too, in the flicker of heat as he'd checked Sam out. Or it'd looked like he'd checked Sam out, anyway.

Interesting. Enough for Sam to toss away his sole weekly day off. It would mean rearranging his entire schedule, coercing Franci to do Dad's grocery shopping, praying that their youngest sister's math teacher didn't call to demand yet another after-school meeting.

Arch scowled, sitting so that he could swap the prosthetic leg he used for diving for the one he wore for day-to-day use. "What if I'm busy Tuesday?"

Ha, right. The Coast Guard veteran did nothing but dive in his spare time. Usually with Sam. Archer was a couple of years younger, but the two of them had grown up down the block from each other. They'd been close since they were young enough to spend their days building driftwood forts on the beach.

"I'll pay you double time," Sam said.

"I know you will," came the grumbling response. "You'll buy me dinner, too."

"You got it." Though Archer wasn't the person Sam wanted to share a meal with.

He didn't normally socialize with customers after hours but was tempted to make an exception for the Irishman. He was dying to know what was in the letter he'd kept below the till, and to read the rest of the places on the list in Kellan's wallet. It spoke to his inner adventurer, the one who'd painstakingly framed and hung maps on the wall in his office, marking all the places he planned to dive in the world.

Had planned to dive.

Lately, he preferred exploring the depths close to home, instead. After his divorce, and then the car accident that threw his family's life into shambles, it felt more secure to stay put.

For his family, for his business, for his admittedly bruised heart.

But maybe getting to show off Oyster Island's underwater paradise to a handsome tourist would add a swath of color to what he'd assumed would be a monotone month.

Chapter Two

The door to Sam's sister's bedroom slammed in his face, followed by a creak and a bone-jarring thump. Charlotte's headboard rapping the wall, no doubt, as his youngest sister threw herself on her bed.

Shut up, Sam, then *slam, creak, thump.* Their evening routine, even on a Friday. Resting his forehead on the door, he groaned. He'd have chosen dessert— or to head to the harbor for an evening out, for once— over an argument about polynomials.

Something thudded against the door. Her textbook, maybe?

Tapping his palm gently on the wood, he sighed. "You know where to find me if you want to take another crack at it."

There were some nights it took everything in him not to agree with Charlotte that she'd never use the

specific math she was learning in twelfth grade. Toeing the *it's about critical thinking* line was downright
painful given he'd thrown his own textbook against
the wall his fair share. He pointed out regularly the
calculations he did for Otter Marine Tours' finances
and dive charts, but his arguments didn't stand up
against her hatred of quadratic equations.

She'd left the dishes in her snit, too, ignoring the
chore chart Sam had posted on the fridge. Not worth
another fight, and his dad was having a rough night
and was in too much pain to pitch in with housekeep-
ing or homework.

It's just dishes.

And making sure Charlotte recovered from her
frustration. And that his dad managed a few hours of
sleep. And worrying about whatever the hell Franci
was getting up to.

*And eventually getting back to living at your own
place?*

One day, but not any time soon.

He owned an apartment up a floor from the shop, a
few houses over in the Group of Six facing the water
at Hideaway Wharf. For the time being, he rented it
out for short-term stays. He had a good barter system
set up—a friend of his dad's owned the local vacation rental company. She managed Sam's bookings
in exchange for tagging along on a couple of group
dives a month. Even nicer was the property manager
not giving him side-eye for living at home again at
thirty-eight.

No one on the island judged his shift in priorities.

Half the island residents had witnessed the wreckage of his dad's truck the night of the accident. They knew the degree of help Greg needed now and that Sam was the natural choice to provide it.

After an hour of putting the house in order, Sam was getting ready for a rousing evening of pajama pants and numbing himself with Instagram reels when his cell buzzed in the back pocket of his jeans.

He took it out.

MK: Your sister needs you

"Sister" had to mean Franci. For all her moments of being seventeen, Charlotte would never sneak out her bedroom window. And if she did, it would be to go hang out in the woods like any self-respecting Oyster Island teen. Nor would Matias Kahale, Sam's close friend and the local bartender, be the one texting him for a rescue.

Gritting his teeth at his inability to keep his fingers plugging all the holes in the family raft, he told Charlotte he was heading out, threw on his hoodie, left a note for his dozing father and went to find Franci.

Her scars from the accident were emotional, not physical, but they were still there, even if she pretended they weren't.

Sam knew he couldn't fix everything. He hadn't been able to protect his family from the pain that came their way. He sure as hell hadn't been able to make Alyssa happy, either. But while there was no point in looking for love again, in the futility of trying to please a partner for more than a few moments, he could support his sisters and his dad. His mom, too, though she was remarried and had her own support system in Winnie.

Ten minutes later, he pushed through the weathered aluminum door of the pub at the other end of the street from Otter Marine Tours. A wall of French-fry-and-beer-scented air warmed his chilled face. Ropes, netting and Styrofoam floats decorated The Cannery, a callback to when it had functioned as a small fish-processing plant. The back warehouse was unused, but the front area, the building's old cafeteria, was a favorite hangout for locals and tourists. Matias had done his research, transforming the place into a comforting mix of nostalgia and island vibes. Sam used to love Friday nights here, before they became associated with having to sop up tears and play designated driver every time his sister decided to tie one on instead of facing her guilt.

He scanned the half-full space for Franci's red curls but came up empty.

Matias caught his eye from behind the bar and jerked his thumb to the back hall.

Sam made his way to the bathrooms. One of the two gender-inclusive doors was closed, guarded by Matias's girlfriend, Mina, who waitressed at the Cannery when she wasn't up to her elbows in clay and potter's glaze.

"Are you taking over?" She flipped her long black braid over her shoulder and smiled sympathetically.

"We've been trying to keep an eye on her. She's been in there for a good thirty minutes."

"Yeah. Tag, I'm it." He knocked lightly, nodding at Mina as she left. "Franci?"

A frustrated curse filtered through the door. "Go back to bed, Sam. I'm fine."

"I wasn't in bed." *And hiding in the bathroom isn't fine.*

"I'll be out in a minute," she said, voice shrill. "Go away."

"I'll wait at the bar."

"For crying out loud. I'm not drunk, I just ate something funny." A strangled sound followed.

Was she crying? He hadn't seen Franci cry once since the night of the car accident.

Sam drew back. "Let me take you home, then. Everyone's worried about you."

"Mati needs to stick his nose in someone else's business."

"Like I said, I'll wait for you."

He emerged from the hallway into the hum of happy activity. Matias waved a meaty palm, and Sam nodded in return. He had a hell of a touch with beer and was one of the few people Sam would trust with his life. The two of them, along with Archer before he'd enlisted, had caused no end of trouble, growing up together on the island.

"She okay?" Matias asked, his dark gaze filled with concern. "She was trying out a new line of sodas for me all night. All of a sudden she turned green, and ran off."

"Sounded like crying to me, but that can't be right. She's blaming food poisoning." He braced his hands on the edge of the bar and sent his friend an apologetic look. "Thanks for texting, Kahale. I'll wait for her until she comes out."

Matias nodded. "Want a drink while you wait?"

"The usual." He caught a flash of pristine, teal-colored Gore-Tex at the other end of the bar. That jacket had to be brand-new. The mark of someone visiting the San Juans who'd done just enough research to realize spring rain came with spring gusts, so an umbrella was useless.

And this particular visitor was otherwise unengaged, it seemed. An empty seat beckoned next to the man who'd spent the day on the periphery of Sam's thoughts.

Kellan Murphy stared at his poutine like it was a science experiment. He chewed methodically, arresting eyes narrowed. A half-finished beer sat on a coaster in front of him. The loneliness of it all struck Sam acutely.

No one understood being surrounded by people but still being lonely more than he did.

Matias lifted a brow and tipped his head toward Kellan.

Sam scoffed at his friend. "I should keep things professional with that one. He just hired me for enough dives to more than cover the shop's monthly rent."

"An excuse to go talk to him and test the waters, if you needed one."

Fair point. "I guess we could hammer out dive sites."

"Right." Matias added cider to the half-full beer he'd just poured. *"Dive sites."*

Flipping Matias the bird, Sam bypassed the three other empty seats in favor of the one by his newest client. He rested a hand on the back of the tall chair. "Can I join you?"

Kellan's dark head jerked up, not a hair out of place. "Sure." He stuck out his hand. "Hello again."

Ha-llo. God, Sam was weak in the face of that lilt.

He accepted the firm handshake. A few calluses. No jewelry. The collection of faded scars on his pale skin reminded Sam of an oyster shucker with terrible technique.

For all the man's urbane appearance, his hands suggested something else.

Curiosity piqued, Sam sat. Matias slid him a steaming mug with a peppermint tea bag in it, Sam's usual at this time of night when he had to dive the next morning.

Could I be more boring?

"Saturdays and Sundays are my busiest dive days," he explained, picking up his mug.

His choice of drink didn't seem to faze Kellan, who clinked his beer glass against Sam's tea. "All good."

They were close enough their shoulders were almost brushing.

The possibility tempted more than any recent indulgence Sam had contemplated.

"You found the local watering hole," he said.

Kellan lifted a well-sauced fry with his fork, a sexy swagger to the crooked curve of his mouth.

Sam nearly fell off his chair from the impact. This guy needed to be careful, wielding a smile like that with no warning.

Mouth dry, he swallowed. "And you went for the weekly special."

"Rules of a new place. Find the pub, order the special." Kellan's gaze narrowed on the chalkboard mounted on the wall where a mirror used to back the bar. "Smart menu, given the size of the kitchen. High-quality mise, most of the cooking in a fryer."

Sam had no idea what "mise" meant, but the assessment sounded valid. "Yeah, Kahale's a smart guy." He cocked an eyebrow. "I take it you know what you're talking about?"

"I do."

No elaboration.

So much for getting any info out of him.

His job. Pastimes. Whether or not he was interested in men in general and Sam in particular.

Sam glanced at the hall to the bathroom and fidgeted with his mug then took a sip. "Hate to admit it, but I'd normally be in bed right now."

"As much as I fancy the idea of you staying out late to flirt with me," Kellan said, "I doubt that's why you came."

Oh. Well, that answered one of Sam's questions. "True. I came for my sister. But I'll take the bonus of your company."

Kellan looked pleased but still cautious about that

response. "'Company' and 'flirting' aren't always a welcome mix, Sam."

"They are for me." Sam decided to clarify because it had taken him a while to identify as pansexual, so the distinction mattered. "All genders welcome. What about you?"

"Exclusively men, to be honest." Kellan's smile was soft, inviting.

Sadly, Sam's brain was too full of Franci's mercurial mood and his fight with Charlotte to have any creativity left to try to impress a smoking hot stranger.

Matias snorted as he pulled a beer from a tap, uncannily reading Sam's thoughts as always. A quick brow lift projected his own. *You have no game. None.*

Not inaccurate. Sam fixed his attention on Kellan, instead. "So, why Oyster Island for your diving?"

"Working off a debt of sorts. I'm after hitting the midpoint—that was the Caymans."

Nothing about that last sentence made sense. Sam leaned in a little. "Say that again?"

Kellan groaned. "Sorry. If you didn't catch it the first time, a second won't fix it. What I meant was I hit the midpoint of paying off my debt when I was in the Caymans. 'After hitting.' I usually remember to lose some of the Irish so people can understand me, but I must be tired."

Sam was charmed. "You arrived today?"

"Yesterday. Spent a night in Seattle first."

"So…" He did the linguistic math. "You're after spending a night in Seattle?"

"Close enough." Kellan's grin lit up the bar. His eyes twinkled. "Next you'll be mimicking my accent."

"And embarrass us both? No thanks."

"Are you going to introduce me to your friend, Sammy?" Francine, right on cue, playing the middle linebacker to Sam's first chance at fun in weeks. He'd been so focused on Kellan, he hadn't noticed her approach. She stood on his other side, not taking a seat. Her eyes were redder than her hair and she swayed on her feet.

"Sammy?" Kellan repeated.

"Just Sam." He took her elbow, steadying her. "My sister, Franci."

Half sister, technically, though they never made that distinction. Having different moms did, however, mean Sam was a hell of a lot older than both Francine and Charlotte, and often felt more like a father than a brother.

She nodded curtly and grabbed a nearby cocktail napkin to wipe her eyes. "The family mess, if Sam didn't already tell you. Ate some questionable leftovers and the whole town's calling my brother. You know how it is."

Matias shot her a protective grimace that might have been an apology. "You need to take care of yourself, Strawberry."

"I'll 'strawberry' you, Kahale." She glared at the bartender. "Seriously, I'm fine now."

Once Sam had his arm wrapped around his sister, he risked a glance at Kellan, expecting judgment.

Their gazes collided for a second before Kellan's

went blank. But in that second, the newcomer exposed something deeper and darker than the jagged crevasse a few hundred feet under the water off Lighthouse Point. Had to be pain.

"Sorry you're having a bollocks day," Kellan said quietly.

"Ooh, this one's adorable, Sammy. You should keep him."

"He's a client, Franci. A little professionalism, please?" Sam tightened his grip on her. "You sure that soda was unspiked?"

"Very," she said, then winked at Kellan, whose face was pink. "Classic diversion, right? Avoid my own embarrassment by shifting it onto my big brother."

"Universal right of a younger sister." Kellan stared at the half-eaten pile of fries. The shadows in his gaze were back. "I'd better get going, too."

Sam winced. "We've ruined your peace. I apologize. Hell of an introduction to Oyster Island."

And to my business.

"No." Kellan's gaze was nothing but sincere. "It's truly no bother."

"Your dives will be one hundred percent drama-free, I promise," Sam said.

Kellan snorted.

Franci elbowed him. "He thinks you're funny. Run with it before he realizes the truth."

"And we're done here." Sam shot to his feet and scrambled for his wallet.

His hot-as-hell client just chuckled and downed the rest of his beer.

Franci's head flopped against Sam's shoulder. "You're my rock, Sammy. Take me home?"

"I'd better before you scare off my new student." He tossed a couple bills on the counter and nodded at Kellan. "Dinner's on me—I owe you for the embarrassment."

His sister's face fell. "I'm sorry. I got carried away."

"Sure, it's fine, love. And there's no need to be so generous, Sam."

"I insist." Whatever this guy's story was, he was mighty tolerant of sisterly shenanigans, and for that, Sam was grateful.

"I owe you, then."

"Consider it a welcome to the island. I'll see you Tuesday, if not before," he said to Kellan before steering Franci out of The Cannery into the cool March night.

"You going to be sick again?" he asked her.

"No. I'm feeling fine now, honest."

"You done crying, too?"

"I *wasn't* crying." Franci groaned as he led her to his truck. "I totally blew your chance with that tourist hottie."

Which might have mattered had Sam actually had time in his life for sex. Hell, even just a date or two. "I think dealing with food poisoning in Matias's bathroom gets you a pass."

She nodded. Under the streetlights, her freckles stood out on her cheeks like the nutmeg his mom liked to sprinkle on the milk foam of the lattes he ordered from her bakery.

"You're pale," he added.

"In case I'm coming down with something, can you put Archer on my dives this week? Or Nic, if he wants an extra shift or two?"

"Yeah, I can figure something out." Archer was almost as protective of Franci as Sam was. And Nic, Sam's part-time employee, was barely out of high school and always looking to make extra cash. Whatever it took to keep his sister smiling. Ever since that police officer had entered the dive shop to tell him the approaching medevac helicopter was intended to transport Sam's father, he couldn't seem to rid himself of his ultrasensitive Franci-alert system. No matter how many conversations got cut short and early, under-slept mornings he had to endure, so long as his family was hurting, he'd be the one trying to mend their wounds.

Kellan woke early on Tuesday morning. Too early. A thin edge of lavender, a brim hinting at slopes and peaks, glowed over the islands to the east. Water slapped the docks, their joints creaking from the waves being pushed to shore by a hell of a wind.

The boat that would take him out on the water was tied to one of those floats.

Dive number one.

Maybe Sam would go easy on him for his inaugural plunge.

He should probably open Aoife's letter—the ones she'd had her executor mail to him in Argentina and the Caribbean were sweet well wishes—but he wasn't ready to see this one, yet. It sat on his bedside table, taunting his avoidance strategies.

With hours to kill until his 10:30 booking, he puttered around the flat, making some sandwiches to share come lunchtime. The kitchen was decently appointed, and there were personal touches throughout the place that hinted at it having been a residence once, not just a rental. Though he took umbrage with the vinyl script quotation affixed over the kitchen window.

There is NOTHING—absolutely nothing—half so much worth doing as simply messing about in boats...

Kellan snapped a picture of it and sent it to Rory, his business partner and best friend in London.

Kellan: Spurious lies.

Rory: Take that back. The *Wind in the Willows* is a treasure.

Kellan: Maybe so, but the boat part is bollocks.

Rory: Hang in there, mate. You'll be back bossing the line cooks around with me in no time.

Right. Rory was counting on Kellan's inheritance, too. Had been the one to suggest they forge a path together, in fact, even before they'd known Kellan would be coming into money. Aoife's gift was getting them where they wanted to be faster than either of them had anticipated.

After finishing the sandwiches and texting a bit more with Rory, he gave up on knocking around his rental, added his e-reader to his thrice-checked backpack and took a centering breath.

Water is clear.

It reflects the sky.

His own affirmations. Simple, factual.

He'd started attending therapy when Aoife got her terminal diagnosis. Nothing to do with the ocean then, just a lifeline. He'd continued to make appointments online while traveling. Recently, he'd been working on strategies to approach diving in what looked today to be slate-gray seas.

Yesterday, Dr. Tan had full-on called him on the carpet. *You need to tell your instructor about your fear ahead of time.*

Not so straightforward, even if he knew it was necessary. His fear made him a liability, and Sam might not want to take that on. Then what would he do to meet the terms of Aoife's will? Head to a different small town or island in hopes of finding a more lenient guide?

Best not to borrow trouble.

And best to show up with a full stomach.

After already preparing lunch, he wasn't in the mood to deal with breakfast, too. Cooking for himself was often a drag after standing at a prep station for twelve-plus hours most days of the week. He'd rather suss out the source of the cinnamon-sugar smells that wafted on the sea breeze into his bedroom window at five a.m. on the dot every morning.

He made his way down the outside staircase and over to the bakery. The air inside carried the heaviness that came from a busy oven, as if yeast molecules were floating around with the sweet, spicy aroma. Not just cinnamon—cardamom, too, and a hint of something savory. Garam masala, maybe.

His stomach growled, and he joined the line. The case overflowed with pastries and sweets. Baskets of bread and shelves of buns lined the rear wall, next to an elaborate espresso machine and a chalkboard menu similar to the one at the pub. Croissants, pies and bread twists caught his eye. He obviously needed one of each. It was an Instagram story waiting to be shared. His mobile buzzed in his pocket, but he was too busy weighing the relative merits of a slice of perfectly golden quiche against those of a bacon-and-egg croissant to answer. He stepped up to the end of the marble counter next to the glass display.

"How can a person possibly decide?" he mused.

"With difficulty," said the middle-aged, white woman running the till. Her blue eyes sparkled with caring-mum energy. "You must be the guest staying in Sam's place."

He startled. "Sam's place?"

"Your apartment." She winced. "I'm sorry—way to be intrusive, right?"

"To some, maybe, but when you're used to a village the size of a thimble, it's par for the course. Didn't realize my dive instructor was my landlord, though. The person from the rental place didn't mention the owner's name." Did Sam not know, either? Or had he not thought to mention it?

"Your landlord, and my stepson."

"Ah, you've a full license to pry, then." He smiled at the woman, figuring he'd do some of his own. "Is Franci your daughter?"

The young woman's smile as she fought through whatever bug she had reminded him so much of Aoife pushing past her chemo nausea, it had hurt his heart.

Sam's stepmom shook her head. "I'm married to Sam's mom, not his dad. Franci came along when Greg married a second time. We have so many family ties, it's a fishnet."

"Complete with catching people?"

"You know it."

"That's grand." Given his parents were as distant as the horizon, Gran had long passed and now his sister had gone to join her, having a family so complicated it took a visual diagram sounded amazing.

He was tempted to ask more questions about Sam, but didn't want to be too obvious. He tipped his head at the sumptuous food. "I've a mind to eat my way through all your offerings between now and April, but where should I start?"

Ten minutes later, he balanced his plates in one hand and his coffee in the other and made his way to a two-top by the window. Gusts rattled the pane. It wasn't bucketing down yet, but the dark clouds on the horizon looked like rain waiting to happen.

Though with diving, he'd be getting wet, anyway.

Under the water.

Clear water. And there were safety precautions, and he could go slowly. He could do this.

Maybe.

He bit into the buttery crust of the quiche, letting the flaky pastry soothe his nerves. If the eggy tart failed, he had a *pain au chocolat* to follow.

Sailboats and fishing vessels bobbed in the harbor, as if they were taunting the wind with a "this is all you got?" The biggest dock, the ferry terminal, was empty of everything except for the cars ready to return to Anacortes. A few people strolled along the boardwalk that fronted the water side of the cozy shops. He could see himself pulling up a chair outside the bakery come summertime, sipping tea and watching the seagulls poach fries off the customers enjoying the chipper next door.

He couldn't avoid the truth—he was lonely. Which, had he expected anything else? He was completely out of close family members who cared to speak to him, and other than Rory, he'd lost his restaurant family after he quit his chef de cuisine position to go on this trip. He'd build himself a new one with his new project, Aisling, but that wouldn't be immediate. He couldn't let the loneliness win while he was here. Making friends in Washington wasn't a permanent solution, but it was better than being alone for a month. And maybe when he got back to London, he'd have shaken off some of the social cobwebs that had collected when all he'd had time for was caring for Aoife and work.

A blur of navy rain slicker, stretched across shoulders as delicious as the quiche, came through the double door leading out to the ocean walk. A blast of cold air tousled the man's hair. Sam took two long strides into the bakery, passing Kellan's table without registering his presence.

Kellan swallowed his mouthful and checked his fleece for crumbs. All clean.

"Sammy!" called out the woman behind the counter. Shoot, he'd not gotten her name. He should have, if he was planning on patronizing the bakery most days. She waved at Sam. "Your usual, hon?"

Sam shook his head and declined politely. Kellan couldn't quite tell, given Sam's back was to him, but it looked like the man was on the hunt for someone. Probably not him, but it wouldn't hurt to say hello.

He cleared his throat. "Good morning, Sam."

The diver whirled. Relief softened his slight frown. "Oh, hey. Just the guy I was hoping to find. You weren't answering your phone, and I wasn't sure where you were staying."

"Uh, your place, it seems."

Eyes wide, Sam pointed at the ceiling. "Upstairs?"

"You didn't know?"

A head shake. "I let the vacation rental company take care of it."

"Ah, you're smart to have an investment."

Shadows flickered across a strong jaw. "Kind of."

Hmm. What nerve had he touched on there? Best to avoid making it worse. "You were looking for me? I didn't get the time wrong, did I?"

Sam's frown returned. "I'm sorry, but the forecast changed overnight. With the tides and the winds, we're going to have to reschedule, or cancel."

Relief washed over Kellan. A reprieve. A damn gift, really. He'd be able to wallow in his coffee and croissant and mystery novel all morning instead of steeling himself for cold and an overloaded nervous system. "Okay. Understandable."

Those clear eyes widened, just a bit. "Most clients get annoyed by short-notice changes."

"The last thing I want is to be unsafe." The last thing he wanted was to do any of this, but Aoife had dreamed venti-sized dreams but had only been given a demitasse worth of time to accomplish them.

So he'd manage his fear, spot some wolf eels, harvest a few sea urchin, greet some otters in a kelp forest, get stuck in that kelp forest—

Not that last one.

Sam was clearly safety conscious.

He shot the man a smile and motioned to the empty chair opposite his. "Feel like sitting? We could pick up where we left off before your darling sister interrupted the other night."

Sam rubbed the back of his neck and finally let his mouth stretch into a bashful smile. "I guess we have nothing but time. I'll grab a coffee."

Kellan's stomach jittered. *Nothing but time.* Possibilities there? This man was the first to pique his interest in a while, and while he wanted to focus on his underwater task, maybe he'd been too hasty on

Friday. Maybe he should save some energy for fun on land, too.

Aoife had added rows eight and nine to her list the week before she'd died, in tiny, shaky script.

> ***Hook up with a local boy.*
> ********Fall in love with reckless abandon.*
> *(The money's not contingent on those ones.*
> *They're for your own good, though.)*

The sentiment made him smile. His sister had regretted not having someone more serious in her life.

Kellan didn't feel the same—he wasn't going to go so far as to fall in love with anyone, not with all the work he had to accomplish over the next few years—but he wasn't about to ignore the first part of the suggestion.

Maybe Sam was exactly who he needed, for more than just his diving expertise.

Chapter Three

"Now *he's* a cutie, honey." Sam's stepmom, Winnie, shook a second helping of chocolate dust onto the top of his latte. "Takes his coffee the same way as you, too. Skim, extra foam, extra chocolate."

"Are you serious?" He accepted the drink by the handle and murmured his thanks.

"That he's cute? I didn't think that was up for debate."

He couldn't deny the attractiveness of the man digging into his multipart breakfast with the zeal of someone who lived for food. A carefully styled, dark brown head of curls. Solemn gray eyes. Shorter and slimmer than Sam, but most people were. And, as evidenced by Friday, so, so kind.

"Is 'cute' the right word?" he asked Winnie.

"With the way he blushes? A hundred percent."

Hmm. She had a point there. But aside from the tendency to turn pink, Kellan was too sexy for a diminutive descriptor like *cute*. Nor could he admit any of that to Winnie, not unless he wanted his mom to find out within the hour. "And he takes his coffee the same way as I do? Weird."

"Well, maybe the chocolate was me, not his order." Mischief glinted in her eyes.

Sam shot her a warning look.

Which accomplished nothing, because she followed up with a teasing, "And he's staying in your apartment."

He sure was.

My apartment.

My bed.

If a person was wanting to be specific.

Which, when it came to love, Sam had learned he needed to be.

Specifically *not* to go there.

Then again, getting involved with someone you knew was leaving wasn't inherently dangerous. It was when you thought they were permanent, and they proved you wrong, that you were left devastated.

"Just think about it," Winnie said.

He backed away from the counter. Her ever-curious expression never led to his life being less complicated.

He turned and walked toward the window table, sparks of excitement in his chest, like he was somewhere new doing something novel instead of strolling to take a seat in Hideaway Bakery. He'd done *that* a thousand times. But he hadn't done it with Kellan

Murphy sitting in the primo seating, biting into a chocolate croissant like it was giving him life. Kellan's lids went half mast, the slack-jawed *oh my God I might pass out* look people usually got when they tried Winnie's baking. If he kissed anything close to how he devoured a pastry—

Chill, Walker. Seriously.

He slung himself into the empty chair, plunking his coffee on the table and cupping his wind-chilled hands on both sides of the ceramic mug. The table was small enough that he bumped knees with Kellan.

"Sorry," he said, scooting his chair back an inch.

"Not a problem." A corner of the other man's mouth turned up. A daub of melted chocolate marked his full lower lip.

Sam had to physically work not to reach over and brush away the sweet remnant. Instead, he wiped his thumb on his own lip in a universal *you have a little something there* gesture.

Kellan dabbed at his mouth with a napkin. His smile turned rueful. "Can't take me anywhere when food's involved. I'm tidier making it than eating it." Sam must have done a piss-poor job of hiding his curiosity, because he tacked on, "I'm a chef."

"Ah, that explains the scars."

Kellan lifted an eyebrow. "Sorry?"

"On your hands." *That I noticed, and now you know I noticed, and I'm not sure I* want *you to know I noticed...* "Never mind. You should see me after family rib night."

"Mmm, you had me at ribs."

For a quick moment he pictured bringing Kellan—or any other date—to a family meal. Franci's teasing multiplied by Winnie's curiosity divided by his own tendency to stay the hell away from anything approaching a relationship. He hadn't gotten involved with anyone since his wife left Oyster Island, and then everything had gotten even more complicated after the car accident. Adding someone special to his life was one too many things.

"Uh, any plans for the day at this point?" He immediately regretted his choice of words. He'd meant to be polite, but no doubt it came across as him fishing in Kellan's personal business. Or worse, fishing for a date.

Kellan's eyes were curious. "All I'd planned was the dive."

Sam groaned. "I'm sorry—"

"No, no." A wave punctuated the assurance. "It's really okay." His tone almost sounded relieved, which didn't make sense. The guy had booked eight dives. Why would he have done that if he wasn't genuinely interested in it?

Unless… Did it have something to do with Sam? Had Franci's little show on Friday turned the man off?

"If there's a problem—"

"Absolutely not." Another convincing promise but followed by a contradictory cringe. "It's grand."

"You don't seem excited, though." Sam took a sip of his drink, trying to swallow down some of his nerves in the process.

"I..." Kellan's gaze darted everywhere but Sam's face.

He was about to prod the chef again, but a twinge in his belly told him to wait. It was a strategy that worked with Charlotte when he needed information out of her. He took another drink, then licked the foam off his upper lip.

He would have sworn Kellan's pupils flared a bit.

Kellan fidgeted with the handle of his mug. "I—"

"You know," Winnie interrupted, sailing past them with an overflowing tray of dishes she'd cleared off a table on the other side of the bakery. "Sam's always off on Tuesdays. And he knows all the good hiking trails, if you're up for an island adventure."

"I did come for an island adventure," Kellan said. But he didn't say it to Winnie. He delivered it right at Sam.

Winnie grinned and carried on her way.

"Ignore her," Sam said. "She's merciless when someone eligible comes to town." He groaned. "Not that I know you're eligible." The back of his neck was as hot as his coffee. "Hell, I'm sorry—"

"I am. Eligible, that is."

"I wasn't meaning to dig." Even a deep breath didn't calm his racing pulse.

Kellan lifted a shoulder. He wore outdoor gear from head to toe, nothing like the soft sweater and crisp jeans he'd worn when he'd come into Otter Marine for the first time. Either suited him. "No point in pretending I'm not single."

"Careful. If you don't keep that to yourself, Winn

will slap a 'ready to mingle' nametag on you faster than she can pull an espresso shot."

"I don't mind *you* knowing." Another flush graced Kellan's sharp cheekbones. "And I wouldn't say 'ready to mingle,' not on any permanent basis, anyway…"

"No need to explain. I hear you." He rubbed the base of his finger where he'd once worn his wedding band.

One eyebrow cocked, attention fixed on Sam's habitual motion. "Married?"

"Not anymore."

"I'd say that's rotten, but without knowing the particulars, I could be way off."

Sam sighed. He didn't want to hash out the blessings and curses of his divorce, not with the most interesting person to set foot on the island since his ex left.

"Winnie was right about one thing—I am off on Tuesdays." And since he'd rearranged his schedule to make room for the dive, shifting the grocery shopping and rescheduling a meeting with Charlotte's calculus teacher and arranging for his dad's kind neighbor to drive him to a doctor's appointment, Sam was actually free for six whole hours.

This could be good. Some fresh air. Intriguing company. The chance to get Kellan to disclose what was bothering him about the dives without any interruptions.

"*Would* you like to go for a hike?" Sam asked.

Kellan paused with his spoon in his coffee, fingers stilling mid stir. "Yes."

A simple answer. A theoretically simple activity. So why did it feel more complicated?

Kellan followed Sam out of the water-side door, thanking the weather gods for being on his side. This hike was the right time to be honest about his phobia, preferable to right before walking onto the dive boat.

Sam paused by the boardwalk's wooden railing, looking as a part of the coastal scenery as the barnacles stuck to the rocks twenty feet below. Kellan might have the local fashion down with his own waterproof jacket, but no way did he blend into the rugged, blustery environment. He was tough and resilient in a kitchen but knew he didn't have that *descended from hearty seafarers* air about him. He should have—his grandfather had been a fisherman, for the love of God—but his build was anything but strapping.

Sam, on the other hand, was the living embodiment of the word.

"Forecast is crap, so we should get going." Sam pulled a thin beanie from his pocket and fixed it over his wavy hair. The olive color lent his eyes a mossy tone, soft and deep and full of contrast. Impossible to look away from.

Kellan made himself anyway, examining the bolts on the planking under his feet. "I'm waterproof."

"I'll have you back before the weather turns."

He could hear the smile in the words and couldn't resist glancing back up to enjoy the flash of teeth and happiness.

Kellan pulled out his mobile and drew up Google Maps. "What's the name of the trailhead? I'll meet you there."

Sam waved off his suggestion. "Nah. Come with me."

He strode in the direction of his dive shop. Kellan jogged to keep up, and nearly tripped over himself when Sam veered off course in favor of the ramp down to the docks.

"Uh, Sam? Where are we going?"

"Secret route. We'll take my runabout."

Holding in a groan, he gritted his teeth and followed. The ramp bounced and squeaked with each of his steps. "Runabout meaning a boat?"

"Outboard and proud." Sam's laugh rang across the water. "I should put that on a T-shirt and sell it at the shop. But yeah, the fourteen-foot beater over there is mine."

Beater. The boat docked next to the shinier, longer dive vessel looked worn, all right. Dents and scratches and a bit of water gathered under the three bench seats.

"I don't use it for shop business," Sam explained, unlocking a metal box affixed to the dock and riffling through it. He pulled out two orange floater coats. "That, I save for the *Oyster Queen* or the zodiac. But you're not paying today, so it counts as personal use."

Kellan blinked, accepting the offered life jacket. "Sure it's seaworthy, like?"

"She's never let me down."

"If you say so."

Sam's eyebrows furrowed. "We don't have to go. If you'd rather drive across the island, we can do that. My way's more fun, though."

He held in another "If you say so." If he was going to have any luck succeeding at diving, he needed to get in a boat. Even if this one was half the dive vessel's size and looked ready to capsize.

Sam gestured for him to climb in and sit on the middle seat.

With two ginger steps, he entered the craft, keeping his weight low. Given the half-inch of water in the bottom, he was glad to have put his waterproof walking boots on this morning. Probably would be good manners to face backward, since Sam would be steering from the rear bench, so he sat smack in the center and forced a smile.

"Once we get going, I'll pull the plug and drain the water," Sam said. "It's just residual from the downpour we had yesterday morning."

Kellan's pulse jumped. "Pull the plug?"

"Easiest way to get the water out."

"Is it, now?"

Sam smiled reassuringly. "We won't sink, Kell."

His head jerked up at the nickname. Other than Aoife, everyone in his life called him Kellan or Chef.

Sam's gaze, already concerned, narrowed further. "Sorry, I should have asked if people usually shorten your name."

"No, but it's fine."

"Cool. Wouldn't want to make you *more* uncomfortable."

"I'm not—"

"Yeah, you are." Competent hands untied the front rope. Sam straddled the driver's seat, one big foot on either side of the bench, and started the motor.

It purred smoothly.

For now.

Sam unclipped the back rope and put a hand on a lever on the side of the motor. "Ready?"

Kellan nodded, clutching the edge of the cold, metal seat.

With a click and a thunk of the motor shifting into gear, they were moving. Sam's right knee wasn't too far from Kellan's own.

Hmm. So there was one bonus to boats after all— close quarters.

"It's only a fifteen-minute ride," Sam said. "But it's a pretty one."

Was *pretty* the right word for the bold colors slashing through weathered, muted tones? It was similar to the Irish coast, but wilder in some way. Steel gray water lapped against craggy beaches and cliffs near tightly packed stands of evergreens. The occasional house stood guard.

"Closer to awe inspiring than pretty," he murmured.

Visually rich and riveting, to be approached with a healthy dose of respect.

Or in his case, an unhealthy dose, bordering on phobia.

Which can be managed with the right strategies. I can do this.

Once Sam cranked the boat motor to full bore, it

was like talking over an industrial kitchen fan—he had to yell to be heard. After having to repeatedly shout a few initial questions about how long Sam had lived on the island—his whole life—and how long he'd been running the dive shop—for thirteen years—Kellan shot him an apologetic smile and gave up on small talk.

Of course, that gave him all sorts of time to circle back to the depth of the water under his feet, separated only by a thin layer of aluminum. The boat didn't so much cut through the waves as it bounced over them with a rhythmic up and down, punctured by the roar of the motor. His soles vibrated with the impact.

If a person was prone to flights of fancy, they could easily picture the force of impact busting through one of the seams.

His pulse picked up until it was doubling the tempo of the *bang bang bang* of the bow against the swells. Shite. There was no point in waiting to discuss this.

"I'm afraid of the ocean," he yelled.

Sam's eyebrows flattened, parallel to his beanie. He leaned closer. "What?"

"Deep water. Not seeing the bottom. I... I hate it."

Cranking the throttle back to near idling, Sam straightened. Empathy softened his green gaze.

The slower revs of the motor meant they'd be able to hear each other better, but it stopped their forward motion. The tidal current, flooding against them, carried the boat backward.

Kellan inhaled deeply. "You didn't have to stop. We'll never get to the trail this way."

"But if you're afraid… Do you need me to turn around?"

"No. I want to go hiking, to see more of the island." He also didn't mind spending more time with this man and his caring, perplexed expression.

They drifted along in the water. A sleek, dark head poked out of a ripple and stared, silently judging Kellan. *Look. It's easy to go under.*

"You can keep going," Kellan prodded, neck crawling from being watched by Sam *and* the seal.

Sam shook his head. "I need to understand. If the water scares you, how were you planning to manage *eight* dives?"

"With months of counseling under my belt."

"Therapy's great, but…" Sam ran a hand down his stubbled jaw. "Why diving? If it scares you?"

"Long story." He hesitated, feeling the boat rock gently in the current, his stomach along with it. "I owe my sister."

"The debt you mentioned?"

"The very one." He'd doubted her for so long, what had appeared like a lack of ambition and faffing about with game apps. So to be given all the money she'd been covertly making and squirreling away in investments and portfolios… So, so many pounds. Enough to cover the costs of Aisling and then some. He'd never listened to her. Never believed her. Only saw the mercurial dreams and judged her for not sticking to a plan. Too embarrassing to admit all that, how much of a tool he'd been. But he had to tell Sam something. "This was supposed to be her trip."

"Oh yeah?"

"She would've loved this." How much the rickety boat resembled their granddad's, the risk of pissing rain, Kellan being inches away from his hot boat driver slash hiking guide...

"May I ask why you're doing it instead?" that hot boat driver asked.

A lump filled his throat. "She's gone. Cancer."

Sam swore, apologetic, just loud enough to carry over the water slapping the hull.

Kellan lifted a shoulder. Sympathy or not, he could tell Sam wasn't going to go through with teaching him to dive anymore. "I understand that you can't administer my test."

Sympathy hardened to determination. "No, that's not what I meant. We're going to need to talk about this more, do some problem solving."

"Okay..."

"But fear or not, if you need to learn how to open-water dive, I will make that happen."

Kellan's heart lifted. "You will?"

"It'll be my pleasure."

Sam couldn't possibly understand how much that meant. Kellan couldn't fail. Not Aoife, or Rory, or himself. And with Sam on his side, he was starting to believe it was possible.

He was in competent hands.

Generous, too.

It'll be my pleasure.

Kellan smiled to himself. He had a monumental task to complete while he was here.

But at the same time, he was up for whatever pleasure Sam Walker had to offer.

Chapter Four

Sam led the way along the shore, mind racing. He'd invited Kell on the hike for fresh air, company and the chance to get the man to disclose what was bothering him about the dives without any interruptions.

Well, mission accomplished. The chef, with his gorgeous jawline and gorgeous accent and unbelievable fear, had spilled his guts before they'd even gotten close to shore. But instead of feeling satisfied, Sam now had more questions. He would have to spend the hike figuring out how to get his client underwater without putting either of them at risk. They couldn't go from zero to diving, not if he was going to keep them both safe. And the best way to create a safe situation was to get to know even more about the man.

Kell jogged ahead of him, balancing on the logs

thrown up against the shore. "This place is magical. The silence is thunderous."

The *th* came out short, just a *t*.

Fine, Winnie, he's "cute."

"Was it worth taking the boat?" Sam asked. Most people accessed the area through a narrow, paved offshoot of the circle road, but he always chose the water route if he had the option. Slowly approaching the shore never failed to fill his soul—the scrape of aluminum on rock, the promise of something new to discover.

"Ha, maybe. We'll have to see what we find."

"You almost read my mind. I was just thinking about how I usually come across a treasure or two."

Kell teetered on a narrow log and caught himself by flinging his arms wide. "Like what?"

"Sometimes, it's as simple as stress release. Occasionally, something miraculous like a glass fishing ball." Today, the discovery was Kell and his fear. It felt both terrible and wonderful. He hated to think of someone being so afraid of the ocean. He was also excited to be let into a part of this man's world.

Nor was he the only one finding new things. Now that they were on land, Kell bounced along like an excited puppy, poking around the line of logs where beach met brush.

"I'd better lock up the boat before we head down the trail," Sam said before taking a minute to secure the runabout by wrapping a chain around a boulder at the high-tide line.

The second he was done, Kell flagged him over.

Kell's eyes, almost the color of the overcast sky, were free of the shadows that had flitted there during the boat ride. He stood on a log, a lanky, relaxed king of the castle.

Grinning, Sam jogged across the uneven surface. "My friends and I used to play tag on the rocks when we were kids. Or 'the beach is lava.'"

"Sounds like a recipe for falling and a concussion."

"Once or twice," he admitted. "And a broken arm for Franci. I was twenty by the time she was old enough to keep her balance, but it was impossible to say no when she begged me to play."

"I was an older brother, too. Not as much of a gap as you and your sister, but still. I moved to London for work long before Aoife was able to follow. I tried to indulge her whenever I traveled home." Kell pointed at a patch of spindly, green vegetation. "Is this area fair game for foraging?"

Sam nodded. "And sea asparagus is delicious if you know what to do with it."

"I just might." Whipping a Swiss Army knife out of one pocket and a small shopping bag out of the other, Kell set to harvesting his find.

The guy might be afraid of the open water, but he was clearly familiar with its bounty.

And bent over, he was showing off some seriously tight glutes.

Sam forced himself to turn around, sit on the nearest log and stare out at the choppy water instead. A hint of Kell's clean scent blew around him, mixing with the salty air. He palmed the log and pressed his fingers against the chilled, weather-worn wood. The only thing he needed to focus on when it came to his newest client was how to get said newest client forty feet below the surface without panicking.

I was an older brother. Kell had lost his sister, and diving was going to help preserve that connection somehow.

Something squeezed in Sam's chest. His family often caused him no end of grief, but losing Franci or Charlotte? Unimaginable.

"How long have you felt nervous around open water?" he asked.

"It's never been my favorite thing. Got worse when we almost lost my granddad in a fishing accident," Kell said.

"Shoot, sorry. That would do it."

"It's not the whole story, though. I tolerated boats enough, even up until a few years ago. But when Aoife was diagnosed, I started fixating on things I couldn't control. I've worked through a lot of it with my therapist, but not so much with the water thing."

"We'll start small," Sam said. "Wading, even. And then snorkeling. There's a calm bay on the other side of the island. If we hit it at high tide, we could float over the reef there, maybe see some things worth seeing without being much deeper than you would have experienced in the Caymans."

Jealousy flickered. Getting to travel unimpeded, diving all over the world? He'd done it before. Damn, he missed his annual trips with his dad.

The suggestion of starting slow but steady didn't

even earn him a glance. Kell focused on his careful cutting and picking. "Are you a cook, Sam?"

A laugh bubbled up. "I try. My dad's out of commission most nights, so it falls on me. But I'm really good at sticking pasta to the bottom of a pot."

Kell straightened. There was a strength to him that made it seem like he took up more space than he actually did given his average height. And the compassion in his gaze was a gut punch. "Salt your water well, and keep it at a rolling boil," he said gently.

"We should probably prioritize your salt water problem over mine," Sam said.

"I reckon there's not much worse than wasted pasta."

Sam recognized the attempt at a subject change. He took a breath. He knew he tended to jump into solving problems for people. He did it all day long with Charlotte, Franci and Dad. And he would need to figure out a way to safely introduce Kell to open water. It didn't need to be right this second, though. They had all day to figure out the best first dive training step. Might as well go along with Kell's need for a diversion.

"Is that what you cook? Italian?"

"Not really. I mean, I can. But I focus on seasonal ingredients. That's why I moved to London—when one of the restaurants on the World's 50 Best list offers you a job, you don't say no, even if it means missing home. But that restaurant was never going to be mine, you know? And when Rory—my best mate—and I open our new space, it'll be anchored in our childhoods instead of having a British focus. Handy that both our grans were named Aisling—makes picking a name easy."

Kell wasn't smiling like Sam would expect from someone talking about their life's dream. The guy just looked... tired.

"What are you going to do with those?" Sam asked, pointing at the fresh-picked greens.

"Depends on if I can find some fiddleheads to go with them."

"I can find you some." Sam did not mind the idea of following the chef through the forest as he poked around hidey holes looking for the right type of fern tips.

A strong hand pointed toward a break in the woods. "Is that the path?"

"Yes. Want me to lead the way?"

"I've got it. You can tell me if I'm going in the wrong direction."

Kell strode up the beach with the surety of someone who'd walked on rocks a thousand times.

"I've never cooked with fiddleheads, but my mom's made them into a pesto before." Not being much of a cook himself didn't stop Sam from loving food. "She and Winnie use local ingredients where they can."

"She works in the bakery, then?"

"Yeah. They own it together." And she'd love nothing more than to meet Kellan, especially if she knew the man was reeling Sam in with the skill of one of the island's best fishing guides.

"If I run into her, I'll have to offer to trade some

recipes." Kell hung back so that they were walking side by side. He rubbed the back of his neck, gaze flitting from Sam's face to the shoreline. "Whatever I decide to cook tonight, would you like to join me for supper?"

His pulse leaped for a second. It wasn't every day a thoroughly adorable tourist asked him on a date.

Except I don't date.

But...wouldn't a meal with someone temporarily visiting the island be safe enough? "I'd be a fool to turn that down."

"Something tells me you're not a fool, Sam Walker."

He'd been accused of that very thing once or twice or a thousand times prior to his divorce.

By noon, Sam was steering his runabout back to the harbor. For Kell, the forest had brought all the fiddleheads he'd ever want, even with being careful not to take too many from one plant. For Sam, it had brought hours of watching Kell's hiking pants stretch across his tight ass every time he bent over to trim tender shoots off lady ferns.

The chef had been up for some hard hiking amid his foraging. They'd both shucked their jackets and tied them around their waists hours ago, and the back of Kell's T-shirt had a sexy, sweaty patch between his shoulder blades. They'd spent the time chatting about life in London versus Sam's tiny island home, and all the hard work they'd both put in with their respective businesses. He felt like one of the pieces of sea sponge littered on the beach—sopping and saturated with facts and insight into the work ethic and passion for food and culture that made Kellan Murphy tick.

He also sensed there was so, so much more going on. Kell had made no further mention of his sister who'd passed away, beyond telling Sam about his plans to dive next in Japan and Australia. If Kell was dealing with grief so big he'd developed a fear of the water, was it really realistic to think he could address it in the relatively short time they had together?

Not that he wanted to force Kell to talk about something he wasn't ready to reveal. And on a personal level, Sam was happy to take Kell's story in whatever order the man felt like telling it. He didn't feel the need to rush. Waiting, getting fed little tidbits, bite by bite, was almost exciting. Maybe he should be in more of a hurry—Kell wouldn't be on the island forever. But how often did Sam get the opportunity to be indulgent?

Slowing the boat as he approached the marina, he lifted an eyebrow at his passenger. Fewer worry lines bracketed the magnetic gray eyes than on their cruise out to the trailhead. "Boat ride was easier on the way back than the way there?"

"Always, when something's more familiar. And return trips usually feel shorter."

"Let's use that as a strategy for your dives, then. We'll familiarize you with the specific area where we'll do a starter dive." Sam paused, piloting in reverse into his reserved slip and cutting the engine. "Though this whole enjoying-the-shorter-return-trip thing—I'm not sure I like you wanting less time in my company."

He meant it teasingly, but Kell's face fell.

"Oh, that is not it, at all."

So quick to clarify. So firm. Boosted a guy's confidence.

After clipping the stern line to the dock, Sam got out and dealt with the bowline. His passenger stayed in the boat, fingers white against the raised edge of the dock.

"You're all tied up. Boat's not going anywhere." Sam reached out his hand.

Kell took it, gripping tightly as he stepped onto the bench seat and then the concrete decking.

He didn't let go.

Sam had almost forgotten how good it was to savor the weight of another person's hand in his. How good would it be to hold all of Kell? Or after it got dark, to throw the floater coats on the dock, lie down, and watch the stars, tangled in each other?

"Were the stars pretty in Ireland?" Sam blurted.

Kell shot him a curious look. "Uh, I suppose."

Heat crawled up the back of Sam's neck. Any minute now, Kell would release the grip, step away...

He didn't, though. Squeezed a little tighter, in fact. "Why do you ask?"

"They're good here," Sam said, fumbling to cover his awkwardness. "No light pollution. If you like that kind of thing."

"I think I would like that kind of thing very much, depending on the company."

My company?

Kell looked up at the overcast quilt of clouds. "Shame it's socked in. You could've showed me after supper tonight."

"I'm sure there'll be one clear night in the next few weeks," Sam said.

"Count on a night of showing me the stars, then." Kell seemed to check himself. "If that's what you were getting at."

"It was. Stargazing isn't as good alone."

The smile he was quickly starting to crave faltered. "You probably say that to all the tourists."

"I really don't."

"I mean, it would be fine if you did. No judgment."

Kell finally unwound his fingers from Sam's and put his hands in his pockets.

Sam's heart sank. Kinda ridiculous—what business did he have getting any sort of attached to someone not local?

Really, his ex-wife would ask him what business he had getting attached to anyone, given how their marriage had fallen apart.

"I know," he said. "But along with all that work I was talking about earlier, and helping my dad and sister after their car accident? I was fresh off my marriage imploding, too. It left me…" Damn, did he want to get into this?

"I can only imagine," Kell said, giving him the out.

He didn't need it. "Shaken might be the word."

"Are you still?"

"Yeah." He shoved his hands in the pockets of his jacket.

"But stargazing's okay?"

Sam nodded.

"Sammy!" Charlotte bolted down the ramp, a blur of black sweatshirt and leggings.

Kell took another step back from Sam.

She stomped toward them, face red in the shadow of her raised hood. She was a redhead like Franci, and turned pink at the slightest provocation. "Where have you been? Why aren't you answering my texts?"

Concern jolted through him, and he pulled his cell from his pocket. "We were out at Buoy Point, over the hill where the service is spotty, and—" He groaned at the string of unread messages, from both his sisters and his dad. "The hot water tank? Seriously? It's like the plumbing in the house has a vendetta against me."

Specifically against Sam getting to have a nice meal made by a sexy chef.

No. Be optimistic. He could get it all fixed and still make it to dinner.

"I cleaned up as best as I could. And I made Dad sit. Well, Franci did. Dad wasn't listening to me." She had that little-girl edge to her voice, the one that sneaked out when she was feeling vulnerable or upset with herself. "I put towels down before the water made it into the pantry. And Dad showed me where to turn the water off."

"Damn, Charlotte, that wasn't your job." He pulled her into a hug. "You did your best. We'll go figure it out." He looked at Kell. "I'll have to meet you back at the apartment for dinner. Can I bring anything?"

"Just yourself." The long slow grin warmed Sam all the way to his toes.

Even though they'd just spent a bunch of hours together, he felt a pang in his chest as he watched Kell head up the ramp alone, carrying his forest bounty in a net sack.

Charlotte stood with her arms crossed over the logo of her hoodie, toes tapping impatiently while Sam rushed to lock away the floater gear and finish securing the boat.

"Who's that?" she asked.

"A client." He didn't want to get into it with his younger sister. For all the advice he doled out to her, he didn't need it coming back.

Her face screwed up. "Since when do you have dinner with clients?"

"Since one invites me to join him."

She scanned the runabout and the *Oyster Queen*. "You didn't take him diving, though."

"Not today." He slammed the lock shut on the equipment box and stood. "Let's size up the damage. We'll probably have to order a new hot water tank." He should have time to do that and get back to Kell.

"Cold showers?" she exclaimed, her face scrunching as if he'd suggested she bathe in black water.

"We'll see what we can do," he said. "Worse comes to worst, we can shower at the shop. Or maybe Mrs. Chang would take pity on you and Dad." Though their dad would struggle without his mobility devices.

"Maybe your 'client' would share his." She put some epic emphatic quotes around *client*.

"Charlotte." He glared at her. "It's not like that."

"His accent is dreamy."

Agreed. He shot his sister a beleaguered look.

"Does he live in Ireland?" she asked.

"He doesn't, but what's with the third degree?" He started up the ramp, and she scrambled to catch up until she was walking at his side.

"You haven't gone out with anyone since Alyssa left," she said, voice small.

"That you know of." He nudged her with an elbow. "You worried about me seeing someone, Charlotte?"

"No. What do I care?" It came out in that particular teenage tone that she'd picked up around the age of twelve.

The one that meant she cared very much. In this case, about Kellan Murphy living abroad.

He put a hand on her shoulder and squeezed. "Dinner or no, I'm not going anywhere."

His roots on Oyster Island had broken up his marriage. He certainly wasn't going to make the same mistake with someone new.

That was the beauty of Kellan Murphy: a meal. Maybe some stargazing. No need for Sam to choose between love and his home.

Kellan stood at the meat counter of the small grocery store, debating which kind of sausage would best suit the fiddleheads he planned to put in a pasta for Sam. Six flavors were stacked in the refrigerated case, each demanding serious consideration.

Sam demanded serious consideration, or at least a well-crafted meal.

He tapped his fingers on the glass case, weighing the merits of asiago and red pepper versus chorizo.

"Tough decision?"

Kellan turned toward the gruff voice. The chef from The Cannery stood five or so feet away, a shopping basket dangling from one of his beefy arms. His dark hair was gathered into a short tail, and between his bronze skin and last name, Kellan wondered if he had Pacific Islander heritage of some kind.

"Oh, hello. Kahale, right? Matias?"

His decent memory for names earned him a nod.

"Ran out of a few things for service?" Kellan motioned to the other chef's random collection of five bags of locally grown arugula and a canister of polenta.

"Yup," Matias said. "I looked you up. I like your approach."

"To food?"

"No, to philosophical debates." The response was drier than the tin of ground corn. "Of course, to your menu. Fussy, but precise. Even though I pay my rent by slopping gravy on fries, I do get precision."

"And they're sinful enough to require a visit to the confessional."

Matias's dark eyebrows lifted and he laughed. "You sound exactly like my grandmother. All you're missing is a rosary."

"Packed mine away long ago, much to my mum's dismay." To say the least. "She's a nun, like."

"What, now?"

"A nun. My parents…" He sighed. "It's complicated. My dad being a cheating wanker, and a divorce that left my mum reeling. She's an only child, so she turned to the church for support. Eventually decided she was being called to join an order, of all things. So I don't hear from her much, except when she calls to say that she's lighting candles for me."

"Because you're gay?"

"No." That was his dad's side of the family. "She somehow manages to jibe her faith with me being queer. The prayers are in hopes I'll drag myself to mass."

Matias nodded. "Same with my oma. I swear she keeps the wax industry in business."

"My gran did, too." Also out of sincere love, not disagreement with who he brought home to supper. God, Kellan missed her welcoming table. His parents had always been distant, but not Gran. He'd learned everything he knew about hospitality from her and hoped to infuse that spirit into Aisling.

Kellan scanned the sausages again. They looked delicious but weren't exactly what he was looking for. "You wouldn't happen to have a meat grinder and sausage stuffer, would you?" Before Matias could answer, he shook his head. "Never mind. It wouldn't have time to chill."

"What wouldn't?"

He pointed at the pork butt. "If I had access to a

grinder, I could get that and chicken thighs and make my own sausage with the exact right seasoning to go with my fiddleheads." And be obvious about trying too hard. "But it's pointless to make a few, which is all I need."

"Sounds like something my customers would like."

"I've never had any complaints."

Matias held up a hand to the butcher, who came over and asked what he wanted. "The pork butt, please." He turned to Kellan. "How many chicken thighs?"

"Ten, but what are you planning?"

"I have a meat grinder and sausage maker I inherited with the place. Show me your recipe, and you can take however many you need for your own dish," Matias said.

Kellan blinked. "Really?"

Lifting a shoulder, the towering hulk of a man smirked before accepting the wrapped packages of meat from the butcher. "I happen to know Sam loves sausage."

Loves sausage?

"You can't be serious."

A snort. "I didn't mean it as innuendo. I meant that he keeps Hills Farms in business." He nodded at the premade links behind the glass.

"How do you know I'm cooking for Sam?"

"Good guess."

"I'd say. And assuming I'd want to come be your line cook for the afternoon?"

"Got something else going on? I have it from the source that Sam's wrestling with a hot water tank."

Kellan's only answer was *cooking supper*, which he'd be better prepared to do if he went along with the other chef's plan.

Capitulating, he flagged down the butcher, who served up an extra cap of pork fat and some sausage casing at his request. "It won't be as good as if the mixture had time to rest," he told Matias, "but it'll still be tasty."

"Are you going to revolt if I put it on fries and cover it in gravy?"

Kellan followed him to the spice aisle. "Not if it's the right gravy."

They conferred about what spices his temporary boss had on hand versus the ones they still needed. Dish components whirled in his brain.

By the time he was in The Cannery's kitchen, jamming chicken and pork through the cast-iron meat grinder, his impromptu recipe was coming together. He could picture the look of bliss on Sam's face when they shared the food—someone enjoying his creations was one of life's biggest rushes.

"You seriously traveled with a jar of preserved lemons?" Matias's tone was closer to amazed than judgmental.

"What else is a person supposed to do when they run across a tree laden with yellow gems on the balcony of their Caribbean hideaway?"

"Probably not pack a jar of them in your suitcase."

He lifted a shoulder. "I've done stranger things for food."

"Well, you wouldn't be a good chef if you weren't intense. And generous."

He shrugged off the compliment.

Brown eyes stared right into his soul. "Sam needs someone generous. Someone willing to give to him for a change."

"Really, it's just a meal," he explained.

"His clients don't usually make him dinner," Matias said.

"Sure, well, his clients usually don't roll in with my issues." Kellan said it under his breath, and immediately wished he'd kept it to himself.

Two black eyebrows rose. "Issues?"

Kellan's mobile buzzed.

Saved by the call.

"Sorry, it might be my business partner."

"Of course," Matias said knowingly.

After quickly washing his hands, Kellan pulled the device from his pocket. It said Unknown Number, but he answered it anyway. "Murphy."

"Kell, it's Sam."

Had his ears been burning? "Oh, uh, hi there." He turned away from Matias and checked his watch. "Everything okay?"

"No." Sam groaned, a low thread of regret in Kellan's ear. "I won't be able to make it tonight. The leak was more of a river than the stream Charlotte described. I'll be cleaning up for a while."

Kellan examined the bowl of ground meat and did

a rough calculation on when he'd be free to leave. Thirty, maybe forty minutes. "Need my help? I've dealt with kitchen floods before."

It was easy to offer to help Sam. Doing anything with the sexy diver would be better than spending the night alone.

"No, thank you." Sam's tone was guarded. "It's...a bit tense around here. Easier to keep it in the family."

Kellan's heart sank at having his help turned down. Silly, that. Sam had every right, and likely a valid reason, not to want an interloper around. It did sound like he had a lot on his plate. On their hike today, he'd skirted around his dad's mobility issues. It had to be a big change for Sam's life, too. He'd found the same thing during Aoife's illness—balancing the need for connection with the need for privacy, for simplicity, for it being easier to do things himself.

"I've an idea of where you're coming from," Kellan said.

"I'm sorry. I hope I haven't put you out too much."

"Don't fret, Sam. Take care of yourself. I'll see you Friday." Disappointment churned, deeper than he'd anticipated.

"Thanks. I appreciate you being cool about it." Sam paused. "I want to ask for a rain check, but I don't feel like I've earned it."

"Put that out of your mind. The rain check is yours."

After hanging up, he sighed and frowned, before remembering that Matias was watching him. He forced the corners of his mouth up.

Matias raised his brows. "He canceled on you?"

"Yes. Dealing with a gusher. Alone, apparently."

"Sounds like Sam."

"At least your patrons will enjoy the sausages." He'd take a few links home, but probably not for the pasta he'd planned. And maybe he could find a different way to be useful. "Want help with that gravy?"

"Yes." Matias wielded his knife with controlled speed. "Want some advice?"

"Depends on the advice."

The blade stilled. "He's worth the rain check."

Chapter Five

He's worth the rain check.

Kellan was counting on that—and that Sam hadn't asked for one out of social nicety—the next day as he made his way down the stairs to the front boardwalk. He carried a covered plate with a piping hot, rustic tart hiding from view. A few fresh desserts were tucked in a paper bag, served to him with a wink from Winnie when she'd weaseled out his intention to share them with Sam. He was taking the chance that Sam was at his shop today, not out on the water. Otherwise, Archer or Franci was going to have a surprise lunch.

His stomach danced as he knocked on the shop's ocean-side door, the staff entrance.

Maybe he should've waited to make plans for a meal instead of surprising Sam, but he wanted to use the sausage and fiddleheads while they were fresh.

Or at least he'd told himself that to justify having gone out of his way to see the diver before their Friday appointment.

The shop's boardwalk door swung open. Kellan felt at a height disadvantage, being two steps down from the entrance.

The person on the other side wasn't a handsome divemaster but Sam's sister, Franci. A wide smile graced her lips, the right side edged by a curved pink scar. What was a hint of ginger and a slight wave in Sam's brown hair was a mess of auburn curls on her. And where her brother was all burly, hard angles, she was lush, with soft curves and wide hips.

Similar to Aoife before she'd dropped multiple stone during her cancer treatment. And he was the shite brother who'd found it painful to hug her, once he'd been able to feel every vertebrae and rib on her back, once her cheeks had been hollow instead of round and hale.

Looking at Franci made his chest hurt. Aside from her shape, she didn't resemble his sister. But the attitude? *Oof.* A too-familiar take-no-guff zeal lit her eyes.

She leaned a hip against the doorframe and crossed her arms over her chest. A magnificent black Labrador, thick and square-headed with a luscious coat, stuck its nose past her. But rather than come for Kellan or the food, it flopped down on its arse and stared up lovingly at Franci. Smirking at Kellan, she gave the canine a scratch. "Already knocking on my brother's back door? He usually doesn't move that fast."

"He hasn't moved at all." He was quick to explain. "He had to cancel our dive yesterday. He took me out foraging instead, so I had to make something from our spoils."

"Had to?"

"I don't make the rules," he said.

"There are rules for foraging?"

"There are, actually, but I'm not going to be the boring bloke who recites a list of best practices when the food's getting cold."

Holding out her hands, she nodded. "I'll give it to him."

"Ah, I missed him, then. A shame." Chagrinned, he passed over the plate and the bag of brownies. "He'll know who it's from."

She winked, holding the plate above the reach of the dog's shiny nose. "I bet he will." She tsked at the lab. "Honu, off."

Kellan cleared his throat. "Well, uh…say hello for me."

"Will do. Take care, now."

Turning on his heel, he plodded along the boardwalk, not in a hurry to get back to the mess he'd left in the apartment kitchen. Mist rolled in off the water, spritzing his cheeks with marine air. He leaned his elbows on a wood railing and stared at the ocean's surface. The tide was high, the water deep enough that there was no seeing the bottom, even near the rocky edge of the harbor. The bottomless green hid its secrets from the world.

His stomach twisted, and fear crept cold up his throat. He swallowed.

Water is clear.

A door slammed behind him, jarring him from his thoughts. Heavy footsteps followed in his wake. "Kell! Wait."

He turned.

Sam jogged the short distance of the boardwalk. He wore jeans and an unzipped burgundy hoodie emblazoned with his business logo over a white T-shirt. Simple clothes. Underrated, perhaps. Was anything better than cotton stretched over a broad chest? "Sorry. I'm in the middle of an online meeting with the local tourism group. But Franci should have told me you were at the door so that I at least got the chance to thank you for the food."

"I knew I was taking the risk you wouldn't be there."

"Hell of a risk, given the intricacy of the pie you made." Sam eased against the rail an inch from Kellan's elbow.

Tangy sea air gave way to skin-warmed bodywash and laundry detergent. Kellan inhaled as subtly as possible. The person who made the rosemary soap he'd bought should really branch into a bar named "Sam."

"Tarts can take some neglect," Kellan said. "Just stick it in the fridge once it's cooled off. You can reheat it in your oven."

"This meeting's going to go for a while, otherwise I'd ask you to join me."

"Kind of you, but I'd have been better to warn you I was coming."

"The surprise was nice." Sam shook his head, seeming somewhat taken aback by his own words.

"Or it wasn't, really?"

"No. Just realizing I haven't been surprised in months. I used to be all over novelty. I've avoided it. But with you…" He lifted a hand, pointer finger raised as if hanging on a question, and then reached forward, calluses rough on Kellan's cheek.

Innocent.

Hot as bloody hell.

"Enjoy the tart," Kellan said. *And feel free to enjoy me while you're at it.*

"I'm looking forward to Friday. Are you?"

He aimed for an "I'm trying" smile but didn't quite get there.

"You'll be safe with me," Sam said with another stroke down Kellan's cheek.

He wished very much Sam would lean in and seal that promise with a kiss, but the diver shook his head, muttered a farewell and rushed back to his shop.

All the better, like. Kellan wasn't here to bake delicacies or forage with a smoking hot local. He needed to get in that water and get licensed so that he could finish the rest of his list and establish his restaurant— his family—in London.

And yet nothing seemed more worth doing than staring into the eyes that matched the color of the ocean he needed to master.

* * *

Sam steered his truck around the last bend of the gravel road, palms sweaty on his steering wheel. He'd driven to Kettle Beach so many times he'd lost count but couldn't ever remember being this nervous.

A row of trucks and cars occupied the parking lot, some beat up and dusty, some pristine. Sam pulled his truck parallel to the silver sedan he recognized as Kell's rental. If it was any other client struggling with fear, he'd have predicted a fifty-fifty chance of the person not showing. He'd had no doubt Kell would be there, ready to keep his promise to his sister. And Sam intended to do what he could to help Kell follow through.

He got out and looked around. No sexy chef to be found down any of the trails, poking around for more fiddleheads.

After locking his truck with the wet suits in the crew cab, he hoofed it down the short dirt trail to the beach. All the people belonging to the cars in the parking lot must have been out on the hike to Teapot Hill, because a lone soul occupied the beach.

Sam would have missed the windblown head of dark hair had he not known to look for it. Tousled strands danced in the breeze, just peeking over the top of a fat chunk of driftwood. Kell sat in a patch of dry sand with his back against the snag of wood, a gnarled root ball weathered by salt water and time.

A path cut through the scattering of logs, allowing access to the rocky bay. Sam made his way through. "Aha, found you."

Kell was dazzling, the sharp angles of his face kissed golden by the sun. He lounged in the sand, wearing a Liverpool F.C. sweatshirt and a pair of those capri sweatpants that looked ridiculous on all but one percent of the population—and Kell fell within that lucky few. His posture was casual but dominant, shoulders back in a way that no doubt projected wordless authority in a kitchen.

Physical bravado, if Sam was reading the tense smile correctly.

Kell fidgeted with a strap on the mask and snorkel he held. He braced a hand on the sand and pushed to his feet, brushing off the seat of his pants. "Good morning."

"Sure is. Gear's in the truck." Sam was excited to get Kell in the water, to keep everything relaxed while he worked through his fear. "We'll put the suits on in the parking lot and carry our fins and snorkels down to the water."

Kell nodded and followed Sam to the truck, their steps crunching in tandem on the pebbles.

"This must be embarrassingly easy for you." Kell lowered his head.

Sam leaned against the tailgate of his truck and crossed his arms. "Hey. It's my job to teach people to be comfortable and calm in the water. That's what I signed up for. And a big part of you being comfortable is ensuring you feel safe. I don't mind sticking close to shore. There's as much to see here as there is in deeper water."

"Thank you." Kell's voice was quiet, weighted by

embarrassment. He didn't need to feel that way. The ocean was a powerful beast, so many unknowns. And trusting the unknown was no easy task.

Sam collected the wet suits from the back and then lowered the tailgate. He threw two rubber doormats on the ground for them to stand on while they changed. He passed Kell the wet suit in his size.

"You're a gem," Kell said, then glanced around. "Right. We're stripping down here, then?"

"So long as you keep your swim shorts or underwear on, no one's going to care. There's also a small change area in the bathroom over there, if you're more comfortable with that." The park served as a trailhead for a network of different hikes, and the outhouse and small shower area was nice enough that people had been known to moor their sailboats in the bay and row their dinghies to shore to use the facilities. One of the many topics that came up during the Oyster Island Tourism meetings—the constant complaints that the toilet paper had run out.

"I don't much care about the lack of privacy," Kell said. "I'd rather avoid a public indecency charge, like."

Sam laughed. "I haven't gotten a client arrested yet."

The chef grinned. "No wonder you have such a high Yelp rating."

Kell's hoodie and pants were in a pile on the tailgate before Sam knew what to do with himself. *It's simple, Walker. Eyes on the ground until his wet suit's on.* Not that a layer of neoprene would erase the urge to sneak a glance. A person in a wet suit was one of Sam's go-to turn-ons.

Especially a person with one pulled up to their waist. Flipping impossible to ignore. Fuzzy hair covered Kell's chest, just enough to keep things interesting. He had the shoulders and torso of a man who liked staying active and strong but wasn't obsessed with sit-ups enough to have a six-pack. Exactly Sam's mindset. There was room in life to be heart-healthy and to love dessert, to indulge sometimes.

It was far, far too easy to imagine indulging in Kell.

Tearing his gaze away, Sam concentrated on stripping down and squishing into his own suit, donning the separate hood before grabbing the long zipper pull and yanking it to the top. He kept an eye on Kell, making sure he was managing the tight parts. For all Kell's nerves about being in the water, he had no problem with getting into the often awkward material.

Kell closed his eyes. "On the scale of one to could-pass-for-a-selkie, how much do I look like a seal person?"

"Aren't selkies the creatures that get stuck on land when their skins get stolen?"

"Yes. My gran swore her gran was one."

The bit of family history was as sweet as Kell himself. "And you're nervous the suit works the same way? Once you take it off and I keep it, you're stuck on the island forever?"

Kell grinned. "Ha. After you have to deal with coaxing me into the water, you'll be counting down the days until I leave."

I doubt that.

Handing over Kell's fins, he then stashed their clothes, put the mats in the box of his truck and hid the key in the tire well.

Kell was looking paler than usual, his face a white oval ringed by the black of his hood.

"All right," Sam said, heading for the trail. "Speaking of rating scales, between lounging on a couch and balancing on a razor blade, what's your comfort level today?"

"Mmm, standing on the handle, staring at the sharp edge."

"Good to start at less than ten." Sam squeezed Kell's shoulder, then second-guessed the gesture.

If only they were more than a student and an instructor. It would be easier to provide comfort. Holding hands on the way down to the water, maybe. Or a hug. It didn't seem right to offer one on the job, even though hugs were Sam's go-to for the moments he had to face something he didn't want to.

Kell was steady on the stones as they traversed the dry beach to the wet. Under the crunch of rock on rock, the ground began to fizz with bubbles and the scurrying of tiny crabs. Sam had timed their swim for high tide, so it wasn't a long walk. They stopped at the edge of the sea.

"Water's calm," Kell said, his gaze on his toes. "I'll be able to see the bottom. Today, I can do this."

Tomorrow might be a different story, said his tone.

"All we need to worry about is today," Sam declared. Yikes, when was the last time he'd said that? He had enough worries to fill his yesterdays, today, and a good chunk of his tomorrows. But in this moment, it was true.

"Right." Kell shook his head. "I've built this up too much in my mind. Yes, I'm afraid of the deep out there, but that's not what we're doing today. Come on." He took tentative steps until he was up to his ankles.

Sam smiled. "Stealing my job, being the motivator."

"It's just a snorkel." Kell fixed his mask over his eyes. "I know what I'm doing, I promise."

"I know. I saw your theory and pool scores."

"Fins on first? Walk in arseways?"

"Once we're up to our waists about twenty feet out, we'll deal with our equipment. Then we'll swim over to the reef." The long, thin spit of land curved like a crescent moon into the bay. "If we're lucky, we'll get to spot the octopus in her den, close to the end of the reef."

"Yum," Kell said, then winced. "Sorry. I know—smartest animals in the sea and all that. But they are scrumptious."

"Conservation's a tricky balance," Sam said. "At least I can be fairly sure oysters and clams don't have feelings."

"I could make you an excellent shellfish meal."

Kell followed Sam out to where the tide slapped their bellies.

Cold water seeped against Sam's skin. It would warm in a second, the beauty of a properly fitted wet suit. Kell seemed unfazed by the encroaching chill and set to putting on his fins.

"Going off the tart you made me, I bet you're a genius with bivalves," Sam said, chatting to keep things relaxed. "You'd put me to shame. Though steaming up a big pot of clams and having them with garlic butter is unbeatable. Even I can manage to put that together." Maybe Sam would invite Kell over for a feast one day before he left. "But no way could I replicate that pattern of fiddleheads and sausage you managed. Where did you get that sausage, by the way? I didn't see it at the store."

"I made it in Matias's kitchen."

Of course he had.

"Hang on," Sam ventured, "you used the sea asparagus in the sausage, didn't you? *That's* why it tasted so good."

"Just enough to season it. Did you like it?"

"I loved it. Wanted more."

"Matias has the rest of it. He was planning to use it for a special, I think. I made him some gravy, too."

"Now I know what I'll be doing this afternoon." Sam grinned. "Happy hour."

The corner of Kell's mouth turned up. "Mind if I join you?"

Sam's breath caught. "I would love that."

The chatter occupied them enough that they both got their fins on without Kell seeming anxious. He stared down into the water, his gaze flitting from left to right.

"What do you see?"

"A sculpin," Kell said.

"Not so delicious."

Laughing, Kell turned and pointed toward the reef. "That way?"

"Yeah."

After a deep breath, Kell fixed his snorkel in place and skimmed out into the water.

Sam followed until they were neck deep, stopping when his student did.

"Mask's not quite right." Kell took it off and messed with the left strap. He grimaced. "I'm not used to these gloves."

Sam held out a hand. "Want me to give it a try?"

They were only a couple of feet away from each other. Gentle waves lapped Sam's chest, pulling him up and down with the extra flotation of the suit. He had to angle his toes to keep his fins from pinning Kell's down.

Kell handed over his mask.

Sam adjusted it, staring into Kell's eyes in the process. His mouth went a little dry. "That should be better."

Kell stretched the strap around the back of his hooded head.

Their hands brushed. Thick neoprene muted the touch, but it still gave Sam an electric rush.

Through the clear plastic mask, Kell's gaze latched onto his. "Thank you."

It came out with rough consonants and soft vowels, and Sam's insides melted. The skin of his belly was chilled from the water but beneath, he was a damn inferno.

Kell cupped Sam's cheek and leaned in a fraction.

Leaning in himself, Sam nodded a silent *yes*.

Cold lips met his own, but there was so much heat promised in the press. Sam expected it to be quick, but it lingered.

Of course Kell lingered.

Hazard of the job, probably. Settling into the taste, the texture of something. And his cinnamon flavor and soft lips warranted a feast. Their masks knocked together and Sam laughed, indulging in another salty-sweet nip of Kellan.

A splash of water doused them, an unexpected wave.

Sam spluttered. That was Kell alright—an unexpected wave.

He was worried the reminder of the unpredictability of the ocean would set his nervous student off, but Kell's smile was soft.

He backed away from Sam with a startled laugh.

"For luck," he said. "The kiss."

Sam rubbed the back of his hood-covered neck. "Hopefully you'll need luck again."

Kell grinned, but it quickly faded as he glanced out at the water. After sticking his snorkel in his mouth, he swam off, arms at his side and fins fluttering with small, efficient kicks.

So far, so good. Sam sliced through the water to catch up.

Chapter Six

It was easy for Kellan to swim around the reef, what with the kiss he shared with Sam completely occupying his thoughts.

His heart hammered in his throat.

For once, it was because of the lingering taste of Sam—the craving for more—rather than from being in the water.

Kellan was well aware this swim was nowhere near the equivalent to a dive. He could see every inch of the bottom. But given he was just nervous and not panicking, he was thankful for the exposure, and for Sam's patience.

Salt stung his lips as he followed that long, powerful body along the shaggy reef. Seaweed and grasses exploded between vivid anemones and sea stars. Mussels and barnacles clustered on rocks big and small, edged with whispers of mossy-looking fibers waving in the current. Silvery minnows darted around clumps of sea urchins. Something else that had him dreaming of his cutting board and knives—under the spikes and shells of the pin cushion–shaped animals hid a delicacy.

It was bloody gorgeous out here. Nothing like the colors of the corals and creatures of the reefs he expected to see as he continued his journey across the Pacific and to the southern hemisphere, but the shapes were similar and still teemed with life. Muted greens and browns, dotted with vibrant pinks and purples from the creatures clinging to rocks, were just as beautiful as the more heavily touted tropics.

Sam waved from the other side of a submerged boulder. His big frame moved gracefully in the water, sleek in the tight black wet suit. He hovered on the surface with ease. Kell could do that, too, when he let himself relax. He had so far during this swim. But it was never far away, the knowledge that if he cast out to his left, he could just keep swimming. And then could start sinking and could sink and sink and sink into bottomless depths.

The exact thoughts his therapist encouraged to let pass him by without engaging.

Not only that, Kell had an eager man wanting to show him something. Something exciting, going off Sam's small but insistent come-hither hand motions.

Kell floated over.

A single, thin tentacle curled out from a tiny hole. *Aw.* It was shy. He'd read that some of the octopi in the area were huge. Not this one, though. Clam and mussel shells littered the opening to the hole.

If Aoife were here, Kell would probably make a crack about her sharing the octopus's table manners.

If Aoife were here, Kell would have stayed home, and would be dry and safe in London.

His chest ached. Sadness warred with the warmth in Sam's eyes. The reality of his sister's absence, the permanence of it, twisted into the darkness in the distance until he couldn't untangle reality from the abstract.

It was all too much. He needed to get to shore.

Pointing in that direction, Kell started swimming, his strokes nowhere near as smooth as those that had gotten him out to the reef. The rocky bottom blurred as he churned along the surface, trying to escape the inescapable: he'd never see his sister again.

A hand snagged one of his, gripping tight, slowing him until he couldn't move forward.

Sam was standing, pulling Kell to his feet.

Kell's cheeks burned—why he was insisting on swimming in waist-deep water, he didn't know. His lungs ached for a full breath. He pulled off his mask and ripped off his hood.

A gloved hand cupped the side of his head.

Sam had taken off his mask and hood, too, and his hair stuck up like a prickly urchin's spikes. "Talk to me." His voice soothed. His eyes searched Kell's face. "What happened? Did we go too deep?"

"No." Kell sucked in a breath, fighting the fist

clamped around his windpipe. "The reef was incredible."

"And we barely scratched the surface. The plumed anemones, the soft corals and the wolf eels—"

"Can we see any of that from a beach dive? A shallow one?"

"Yeah, some." Sam's eyes were still dark with worry.

"Let's plan that next."

Sam frowned. "Okay, but...you're not happy."

"This wasn't about that. Promise." Kellan leaned in for another kiss, one that made his toes flex in the stiff-soled diving boots.

Was he being borderline unfair, using Sam to recenter? Perhaps. He should've been belly breathing or counting sensory experiences. But that was pointless when every sense, every breath, was full of Sam. The only touch worth feeling was his lips on Sam's full ones. And sounds, too. Sam's gasp, his breath, his moan. Kellan assumed seagulls were squawking and waves were lapping on the rocks, but none of those noises were making it to his ears for the buzzing as his blood heated.

It was just Sam and the sea, the sea *on* Sam. Kellan bet he carried a hint of the ocean at all times of the day, and was willing to put that to an experiment. And taste? Even Kellan's most sophisticated culinary training couldn't break down something as complex as the flavor of this kiss on his lips, on his tongue.

All Kellan knew is that in kissing Sam, in taking in every second of being this close, he relaxed. No matter what, he wanted this memory. Of Sam, the beach, the kiss. This rugged and beautiful man who matched the wild landscape.

The pain of loss shifted to a dull throb. Aoife might not be alive, but Kellan was, and he was allowed to enjoy his days. In doing so, he was fulfilling her request. But it was about his own desires, too.

His tongue lashed against Sam's, trading need for need.

Sam's hands stroked Kellan's shoulders, his touch dulled through the thick material. It wasn't enough. Kellan wanted to do this in clothes, something thinner where it was easier to touch.

Or maybe one day, no clothes. The possibilities there were beyond tempting.

They parted slowly, reverently.

A touch of amazement rode Sam's face, but it quickly dimmed. He started retrieving the hoods and masks they'd discarded while kissing. "Are you sure you didn't panic?"

"About kissing you? Of course not."

Sam shot him a no-kidding smile. "You were swimming back to shore like you had a shark on your tail."

"I sort of did. I was having a moment of grief," he admitted. "They come and go."

"They do," Sam said, with more than empathy.

"Personal experience?" Kellan hated that for him.

"I've lost a few people over the years. No one as close as a sister." Sam pressed his lips together.

"It's never easy," Kell said. "Even if you're surrounded by family, like you are."

The opposite of me. Losing Aoife had meant more

than losing a sister. He'd not understood how empty *alone* could feel until he packed up her belongings from the palliative care unit.

His eyes stung, and he pressed the heels of his hands against them. "So, diving."

The words were unmistakably tear-stained.

Sam ran his gloved fingers through Kell's hair. "I don't want to make light of your low moment."

"Diving, Sam. Please."

"Well…" His instructor coughed. "It wasn't the ocean that threw you off. That'll make the next step easier, whenever you're ready for it."

"I'm in your calendar for Monday." He dropped his hands from his face. With any luck, his eyes wouldn't be too red. "No chickening out on me, Walker."

"Monday," Sam repeated. "I'm all yours."

If only wishing made it so.

Charlotte and Franci were behind the front desk when Sam got back to the shop, toting the damp suits and fins in a gear bag. Charlotte was hugging her calculus textbook. Franci was in the tall chair, kicked back with her feet on the low half of the counter and eating out of a small bag of Hawkins Cheezies— Cheeto-like snacks she took the ferry to Canada to stock up on.

Nudging Franci's feet off what used to be a pristine counter, he stared at Charlotte. "It's still school hours."

Sam didn't much like being his sister's school attendance monitor, but his dad still resisted taking on anything to do with the island's combined middle and high school. Sam didn't know whether it was grief or embarrassment—his dad wouldn't talk about it—but it wasn't hard to see the connection between Greg being unable to return to his woodshop and PE teaching position after his accident and being wholly okay with Sam staying on as academic point person for Charlotte.

Initially, it had been a necessity—Greg hadn't been able to sign permission forms, and reading screens or print left him with daylong headaches. That wasn't the case anymore. Maybe it was time to talk about rebalancing the family tasks.

Might be nice, shifting back to being Charlotte's big brother rather than her quasi-guardian.

Who was he kidding? He'd still get after her for skipping.

He sent her an "I'm waiting" look.

"It's Friday," she said with an eye roll. "I have my study block."

"Shouldn't you be using that to find a *study* carrel and work on your calculus?"

She glowered. Her gaze flicked to the window that faced the dock. "Fran's helping me with it."

Not by the way Charlotte's textbook was closed.

Sam glanced out the same window. Nothing notable there. Out on the boardwalk, Archer and their part-time deckhand, Nicolas, were cleaning the crab traps they took on some of their shore-based tours. Nic, Matias's cousin, was only a year older than Charlotte—*Oh, hold on. Only a year older than Charlotte.*

Son of a—

"I had to shower at Mrs. Chang's this morning," she grumbled, stealing a Cheezie and earning a squeak of protest from Franci.

"What, would you rather have showered here?" Sam said.

"Why can't we just use your apartment?"

He cocked an eyebrow. "Because it's been rented until the end of the month. You know that."

Charlotte made a face. "I figured you could get out of the contract."

"No, I can't." He sighed. "There's always your mom's."

"Ew. I'm not sharing with my stepbrothers. Not a room, not a bathroom, not anything. There's no space for me there."

Franci and Charlotte's mom lived on the other side of the island with her second husband and a passel of kids; two theirs, some his from his first marriage. As much as it was a loving home, it was definitely crowded. Charlotte had decided long ago that she'd live at Greg's full time.

"I'll be home tonight," Sam promised.

She looked out the window again.

"Seeing something you like, small fry?"

Her cheeks reddened. "I told you, I came for help with math. Franci's better with derivatives than you are."

"Yeah, her C-plus to my C," he said.

"One Cheezie plus one Cheezie is two Cheezies,"

Franci said dryly. "I've got the important stuff covered."

"You, uh, need a hand with calculus, Charlotte?" Nic asked from the dockside door, hands gripping the frame of a webbed trap, his shy smile surrounded by a five o'clock shadow that Charlotte no doubt thought was "dreamy." Oyster Island was small enough that Nic's charmer reputation was well known.

Sam wasn't sure his sister's experience matched Nic's, even if the kid was looking at her like she was the source of the world's oxygen.

"I took it twice so that I could get an A," Nic continued.

"You would do that?" she squeaked. "Help me, that is? Not taking math twice. That makes total sense. I'll probably have to do that. Not to get an A, though. I wish." Her face was so red, it looked like she'd just gotten back from a ten-mile run. Nic's was about the same, though, even with his light brown skin.

"My shift is done." Nic glanced at Sam for confirmation.

Sam nodded. It was 1:00 p.m. on the nose.

"Bring your stuff," Nic said. "We'll go across the street to the library."

Charlotte sent Sam a look he didn't quite know how to interpret. He could still see pigtails and skinned knees when he put his mind to it. Juxtaposing that image with the young woman in front of him made his brain smoke. He wanted to wrap her in tissue paper and protect her from any more pain.

Of all of them, Charlotte had had the least amount

of control over the changes their dad and Franci's car accident had inflicted. Sam had been the only one capable of supporting her for a while as their dad healed from all his broken bones. He wanted to make her life as stable as he could, and God knew her being interested in Nic wouldn't be anything but drama. But he wasn't going to embarrass her—or his employee—by discouraging them from going to the library together.

He wanted to keep believing she was too young to date. She wasn't, not really. He was just cranky and earning the sprinkle of gray hair starting to make itself known at his temples. And yeah, a little bit bitter. Along with keeping Charlotte's life stable, he wanted her to see all of life's possibilities.

Some days it was harder than others, knowing it was possible to be the one left behind.

"Promise you'll deal with whatever you have due for tomorrow?" he asked.

She pinned him with a glare.

"What? I'm the one who keeps getting calls from the school—"

"*Sam. Shut up,*" she hissed, her expression darting between him and Nic.

"We're just going to be at the library," Nic said.

"I wouldn't have expected otherwise."

He totally would have. There was all sorts of trouble that the two could get into.

She waved Nic toward the door. "Let's go."

"I'll have dinner on the table at six. I was going to get takeout from The Cannery," Sam called out to his retreating sister.

He had a daily special of poutine with Irish-made sausage and gravy to try.

Charlotte shrugged. "I might be home."

"Text me," he insisted.

Stop hovering, her eyes said before she disappeared out the door behind her new tutor.

"She's not going to be home for dinner," Franci predicted, licking orange dust off her finger.

"Maybe I won't be either, then," he said. That wouldn't work, though. Dad would end up eating something as nutritious as Franci's bag of cheese-dusted sticks.

"Oh, yeah? Now that you finished that tart, you're going back for more?"

"No. I don't have plans to see Kell again." *Yet.*

He didn't know why he was making excuses. Just like Charlotte had a right to hang out with a local boy who'd caught her eye, Sam could have some harmless, temporary fun with a tourist. The *harmless* part being contingent on the *temporary,* of course.

Franci pointed at the schedule on the screen of the point-of-sale tablet. "Until Monday, when you take him out again."

"That's work, not 'taking him out.'"

Crunch, crunch.

Dropping the gear bag, Sam held his hand out for the Cheezies.

"Those who tease me for buying them don't get to partake," she said, keeping it out of his reach.

"Those who get caught with their feet up at work need to pay a slacker tax."

He reached for them. She squealed and nearly fell out of her chair.

"What the hell?" Archer interrupted from the door to the boardwalk. "Francine, be careful."

Franci straightened and wiped her mouth with the back of her hand.

Arch scowled and walked past to go to the staff washroom. He paused behind the counter. "Francine and I are switching shifts again for the next week," he said with a grunt. "Add her two dives onto the three I'm already working. She's going to take my hot spring tours."

There was no point in trying to read anything off Archer's flat expression, so Sam narrowed his gaze on his sister's flushed cheeks. "Why? You didn't end up having the flu or a cold."

"My back's bugging me. I'd rather not have to deal with hauling around cylinders," she said.

"How bad is it?" Sam asked.

"Just enough that I don't want to dive." Franci smiled assuredly. "I'll be fine, Sam. Promise. I have a couple of chiro appointments booked this week."

Making another low noise of protest, Archer reached over the counter to catch an orange spot on the corner of her mouth with the pad of his thumb. "Missed a spot."

"Th-thanks."

Blanching, he grumbled a goodbye and disappeared into the bathroom. Once Archer had the shower on, Sam wheeled on his sister. "What the hell was that?"

"Less than nothing. I could ask the same about that

Irish dude touching *your* face out on the boardwalk a couple of days ago."

Or kissing me in the water.

"Spying on me?"

"Interfering where you shouldn't?" she rallied back.

"Arch is my employee. And my friend." *And is more relationship-averse than I am.*

"And Irish dude is your client."

"Which isn't an ethical issue. I'm not his doctor or lawyer or anything."

"Just stating the obvious connections, like you were." *Crunch.*

He snatched the bag away and headed for his office. "Don't set yourself up for heartbreak."

"Same same, Sammy."

Chapter Seven

Pitching his cell phone through the front window would just pile on one more problem, but it was sure tempting. Instead, Sam hung up with the plumber and put the device on the counter. His next call was going to be to Alice Chang—they were going to need to impose on her generosity until next week, it seemed, because supply chain issues meant their new hot water tank was stuck in a warehouse somewhere.

Damn it. He had a Sunday kayak tour starting in an hour, and he needed to get out of his mood before then. But the thought of having to explain to Charlotte they had ten more days of boiling water to do all their dishes and showering at the house next door didn't make him happy.

Perspective—it wasn't having to make trips between home and the San Juan Island hospital, being afraid of losing his dad. It wasn't even close to what Kell had gone through with his sister's cancer. It was an inconvenience, an annoyance. Not a crisis. But having gone through a crisis and dealing with their dad's ongoing pain and frustration meant Charlotte's threshold for annoyances was low.

He made the call to their neighbor and then texted Charlotte to come by the shop if she could.

The bell on the door rang. He looked up, expecting it to be one of his kayakers, arriving early.

Kell's gentle smile appeared in the doorway instead.

Even better.

He didn't bother to keep the grin off his face. "Hey there."

His visitor made his way past the racks, stopping on the other side of the counter. He placed a medium-size paper bag on the glass and braced his hands on the edge. The slight lean forward was all Sam needed to read a clear invitation for a kiss.

Mirroring Kell's posture, Sam pressed his mouth against the beautiful, closed-lip smile. He coaxed Kell's lips open, teasing with his tongue, tasting mint and spice. Fingers sifted through his hair, rough and demanding, pulling him closer. Kell teased back, nipping, licking into Sam's mouth, easy strokes of hands and lips.

One of them moaned, and Sam couldn't be sure it wasn't him. Goddamn. He was getting carried away. Reluctantly, he pulled back.

"You know, the first time you came in here, I thought about kissing you."

Kell stepped back and leaned against the map-covered post, eyes glazed. "Your biceps kept me from having a full-blown panic attack when I handed over my credit card."

Sam laughed. "At the time, I thought all you wanted was diving lessons."

"I do want diving lessons. I need my license." Kell's mouth quirked, sheepish. "I might want you, too, though."

"Might?"

"Gotta keep you on your toes." The bag crinkled as he held it up. "But also keep you well fed."

Sam caught a whiff of fresh-baked bread and some sort of meat. His stomach growled. "You don't need to bring me food." He took the bag. "But I will happily eat it."

"If I'm making one sandwich, it's a crime not to make two."

The sandwich was wrapped in wax paper. Sam unwrapped it, revealing a triple-decker of what looked like Winnie's rosemary-and-potato bread, layers of paper-thin roast beef and a rainbow of vegetables nestled between the savory slices.

"You roasted the beef yourself, didn't you?" He took a bite. *Heaven.* There was no other way to describe it. He swallowed. "And what the hell did you do to the horseradish to make it taste like this?"

Kell lifted a shoulder. "I get bored. I'm not used to being alone. Restaurant kitchens are full of people.

And after my shift, if I'm not out with my kitchen staff, well… London's a busy place at night, like."

Their gazes locked. Sam could think of a hell of a lot of ways to keep his guest entertained once the sun went down.

Not guest. Client.

Not that he couldn't be both.

"I'd love to offer to keep you company this afternoon, but I have a kayak tour I'm taking out soon." He took another big bite of the sandwich. Yup, just as amazing the second time it touched his tongue. The perfect fuel for being out on the water, too. "We could rake in money if we offered your food on our day trips."

That earned a chuckle. "I've been known to turn a profit with my recipes."

"Matias can't stop singing your praises," Sam said.

"Glad I was able to help him."

"If you're bored, I still have a spot on my tour this afternoon. It'll be cloudy, but no rain in the forecast."

A wince of regret. "I'd honestly consider it, Sam, but I'm afraid I've a meeting I can't miss."

"Work?"

"My therapist." *Tare-apist.* Yikes on toast, that brogue was hot. "I've a beach dive tomorrow, giving it a lash, you see, and I need to be in fine shape. I'm trying to impress my instructor."

One more lingering kiss and Kell was gone, sauntering out the back door.

Sam stood with his sandwich in one limp hand

and his jaw near to the floor after having the breath kissed out of him. *Impressed?*

Kell had nothing to worry about there.

Kellan got to the beach an hour early on Monday, planning to meditate alone. He'd not told Sam he'd been walking the beaches in advance. Wandering the harbor docks, too. He'd been fitting it in, around all the cooking he'd been doing.

Besides conquering diving, all he'd wanted to do since he got here was feed people. The delicacies of the Salish Sea—and having someone as lovely as Sam to cook for—were lighting a spark in him he hadn't experienced in years. Maybe since he left Ireland for London. He should probably run that by his therapist, too.

Today's beach was a different stretch of rock and water from his snorkel trip, and again it was a stunner of a view. After ten days of being on Oyster Island, he was starting to see beauty instead of doom when he looked out at the sea. He'd take the small progress.

That was likely the key, really. Small things. When he was snorkeling, focusing on one animal at a time had helped take his attention off the vastness.

How long would he last underwater today? How deep would they be able to go? He doubted it would count as one of the four official dives he'd need to take to get his certification. Aiming for even one of them felt like too big a step for today. He still had close to three weeks to get those dives in. Today was just for taking a few breaths underwater with a reg-

ulator, for staring out into the depths without hyper-
ventilating and for not scaring Sam off from helping
him through the rest of the process.

This time, when Sam strolled onto the beach, the
conquering hero ready to tame the wilderness—and
hot as any surf god who'd ever walked around with a
wet suit rolled down to his waist—Kellan didn't feel
clammy and on the verge of retching.

If he got two feet under and decided that was
enough for today, so be it. That would be his best.
Tomorrow's best might be more than today's.

He wanted more than two feet, though. Five. Ten.

And after, all of Sam.

Sam sat on the log next to him and stretched out
his long legs. "Can't beat the view here at high tide."

"It's so quiet. I can hear myself think." Kellan
laughed. "I'm not sure that's a good thing."

Sam paused for a long moment. "I feel the same
way sometimes."

"Do you?"

"Hard not to." His hands tightened on his neoprene-
covered knees. "Work, Dad, the house, my sisters. Not
in that order, of course."

"Impossible choices, sometimes, and you end up
feeling like you're shortchanging everyone. I've done
that, Sam. Been someone's primary caregiver. I mean,
toward the end Aoife was in the hospital, so it's not
quite the same, but I was there every moment I wasn't
working."

"You get it, then."

"Parts of it, at least," Kellan said. "Especially putting off anything fun."

"I haven't had much of that lately."

Kellan wanted to be fun for this man. Mix his life up a bit. He stood. "I'm aiming for fifteen today. Feet, that is."

"That's why I picked this beach. That wall over there is worth seeing at any depth."

He didn't have time to get nervous; Sam kept him busy with pre-dive tasks, checking equipment, doing the maths for their weight belts. It felt like one minute he was squeezing into the rented wet suit and the next he was submerged. Sam was a constant at his side, only an arm's length away under the water as they swam down, down, following the curve of the drop along the promised cliff wall. It stretched out ahead, seemingly endless. Not the lightless depths of his irrationality, but green, shot with sunlight, catching on the microscopic bits and bobs floating through the water.

When pressure demanded he equalize, he knew what that meant. He was six feet down.

A few more kicks, and he'd be at his goal.

He stalled.

Sam paused, too, and checked his depth gauge. No way would he normally need to check here, not with his level of experience. They were barely underwater. The fact he was doing it for Kellan, specifically for Kellan's comfort, proved the kind of man he was. Thoughtful, responsible. Caring. Sam's eyes were encouraging behind his mask. He waved at Kellan. Bubbles rose as he exhaled.

Breathing.

Kellan's lungs constricted, and the regulator felt clumsy in his mouth.

Find something small. He looked at Sam, soaking in the bright encouragement in his gaze. Then he fixated on the wall, counting the different colors of anemones. Pink. Purple. So many in green, small and squat, like tiny wine gums stuck to the granite. Farther along the wall, maybe ten feet ahead and five feet down, a white anemone swayed in the current, the long neck almost crude, the feathery tendrils like intricate fronds. There. Whether it was ten feet or fifteen, that's how far he'd get today.

He caught Sam's attention—well, he'd had Sam's attention the whole time, no doubt, but he reconnected, anyway—and pointed at the graceful animal.

Sam nodded, swimming next to him with powerful but calm kicks.

Kellan met the rhythm, one, two, three...and wow. That was all it took.

The white plume danced in front of his face. He'd have grinned, but the regulator got in the way. He let out a big gush of breath. The hiss in and bubbles out were a rhythm, one more thing to focus on.

Sam touched his arm and held his depth gauge up for Kellan to read.

Wait, was the needle pointing at fourteen? Almost there.

Emotionally buoyed, he let out a titch of air from

his buoyancy control device to sink a little lower in the water, enough to get the gauge attached to his own tank with a long tube to register fifteen feet.

He gave Sam a thumbs-up.

Sam returned the gesture and took his regulator out of his mouth. He said something that looked like *you did it*. Hard to tell exactly because of the bubbles coming from between his lips.

Kellan's panic threatened to ratchet up at the sight of Sam without his breathing apparatus in his mouth, but no, it wasn't a big deal to take a regulator out for a few seconds. Kellan would have to do that on purpose— would have to share a regulator with a diving partner while forty feet deep—in order to pass his course.

Being that deep with no air.

Made his throat tighten while in the comparative shallows. *Shite*.

Taking a deep breath—at least today, he had plenty of air—he motioned for them to go back. Best to end on a high note.

He hit even more of a high note once he was back in the parking lot and half stripped of his wet suit. Sam clutched a towel around Kellan's shoulders and pressed him against the door of his rental car, kissing him like he'd done something truly spectacular instead of just submerging a few feet underwater.

It was the strangest thing, being freezing cold in places but hot in others. He gripped Sam's hips and kissed his lips, his cheek, above his ear where damp tendrils of hair chilled Kellan's mouth.

"We should find somewhere better to warm up," Kellan said.

Sam groaned. "I wish. But I'm working until this evening."

"Too bad. Need help cleaning up?"

Sam's headshake was deeply disappointing.

"I'm off at five, though," he said.

"I might still need warming up by then." Kellan would make sure of it.

"Given your place is actually my place—" Sam's wicked grin hinted at enough heat to warm Kellan for days "—I know all the tricks of the shower."

The excitement of the dive and Sam's promised visit kept Kellan flying all afternoon. He was on top of the world for having submerged fifteen feet below ocean level. Didn't sound like much, but he refused to minimize his success.

After taking a quick kip, he texted Rory.

Kellan: Made it 15 feet under.

Rory: 15 feet closer to Aisling.

Kellan frowned. He'd've liked a bit more fanfare about his personal success before connecting it to the business. He replied with, Twenty-five to go.

Rory: I believe in you.

Rory: You never told me what Aoife's mysterious letter said.

Because I'm being an eejit and still can't open it.
He didn't type that.

Kellan: Nothing earth shattering.

Rory: <ghost hug GIF>

Kellan: Give me 5. I'm going to send you a picture of a loaf of sourdough that outdoes yours.

His mate was religious about feeding his sourdough starter, lovingly named "Harriet."

Rory sent a GIF of Thanos saying "Impossible."

Kellan laughed, then replied with one from *Hamilton* emblazoned with "Just you wait."

He threw on a thick sweater and headed for Hideaway Bakery. The place was doing a brisk business for four in the afternoon. People in need of an afternoon caffeine fix, no doubt. Kellan wasn't sleepy any longer, but his stomach was growling like a cranky feral cat. He snapped and sent the promised picture while waiting his turn, and quickly added it to his Insta story while he was at it. Despite not currently working, he still had a following he needed to maintain for when they did open Aisling.

Winnie was behind the counter, polishing her vintage-looking, meticulously kept espresso machine. That, plus the high-class beans on display—no wonder the coffee was next level. He took a picture of the machine and posted that, too, tagging the bakery.

She turned, and her smile brightened. "Kellan. The day's starting to drag. Spin me a yarn."

He sidled up to the counter and planted a hand next to the tip jar, shifting his weight. "How can you be certain I've any storytelling skill?"

"I have it on some authority that you've been adventuring. Those days always make for the spiciest tales."

"I doubt the adventures I've been on are the kind of stories you're hoping to hear. They're water-related. Entirely lacking in scandal."

She clapped her hands together once. "You made it into the water, then?"

"Twice." Pride curved the corners of his mouth. "Worked up an appetite, too. I'm thinking a scone will set me to rights. You wouldn't happen to have clotted cream, would you?"

"Wouldn't serve it any other way."

She had the comfort food whipped up and arranged in no time.

He picked up the plate and inhaled deeply. "You're a master. Any chance you've a loaf of yesterday's brioche in the back somewhere?"

"Making stuffing?"

"Tempting—those locally raised chickens I saw at the meat counter would roast like a dream—but I've a mind to cook breakfast." French toast. With homemade spruce tip syrup, if he could manage it. He wanted to manage it. He wanted to invite Sam to stay the night.

In Sam's own flat. Bit strange, that.

Hey, feel like sleeping over? In...your bed?

And in the morning, Kellan would make Sam a breakfast that impressed him just as much as anything they managed to do between the sheets.

He shook his head at himself. He was making a whole lot of assumptions about what Sam may and may not want. Kissing him against a car, Sam alluding to sharing the shower—neither thing guaranteed he was interested in sleeping over or breakfast.

But Kellan had still changed the sheets after getting home from his dive.

And it wouldn't hurt to have a loaf of bread in the kitchen.

Winnie plopped said loaf on the counter in front of him. Her eyes glinted. "Breakfast for dinner, or planning for tomorrow?"

"I like to be prepared," he said, unsure how publicly Sam wanted their private business aired.

He pulled out his wallet to pay just as the bell on the door rang.

Awareness rose on the back of his neck. Not a "danger, danger" alarm. He knew, just knew when he turned around that Sam would be there. And sure, something clamored in his belly. A "pay attention, friend" feeling. With a sliver of "this person could become bloody important" thrown in.

He resisted the urge to glance over his shoulder and focused on pulling out his credit card and tapping it on the machine. Winnie's eyes—scheming as they were—locked on a spot over his shoulder, just as five strong fingers spread slowly between his shoulder blades. A few hours ago, those fingers had been threaded through his hair. A few hours from now, they might be on his bare skin.

"Hey, there," Sam said.

"How's she cuttin'?" Kellan rocked back on his heels, pressing into the touch.

Sam's hand stayed put.

Excellent.

Winnie didn't miss it, that knowing gaze soaking in everything around her. Giving her approval, too, a little twinkle of amusement lighting her face as she handed Kellan his receipt.

"On second thought," he said, "mind if I get this scone wrapped up?"

"By all means." She went about putting it in a container.

He finally turned. Sam didn't drop his hand, though, just shifted it to Kellan's biceps. What was it about this man's lit-sea gaze that had him thinking beyond breakfast? Those were the kind of eyes a person could picture in their life, waking up to in their bed, arguing over whose turn it was to take out the garbage.

Except they lived on the other side of the world from everything important in Kellan's world. Everything he had left, and everything he planned to build.

"You found me," he said. "Though this island is about ten meters square, so perhaps it's a coincidence."

"I was looking." Sam leaned in. "Haven't been able to look anywhere else since you got here."

"Sure and you're a flirt, like."

"Our Sammy?" Winnie said. "He's always been too serious to flirt."

"And here I thought I was being quiet," Kellan said ruefully.

"The only person with better hearing than Winnie is my mother," Sam said. "I'm assuming she's not here, Win?"

"Sadly, no. She's home feeding the goats." Winnie handed Kellan his packaged scone. "Rachel will love you, honey."

Sam let go of Kellan's arm and jammed his hands in his pockets, taking a step backward. He shook his head at his stepmom.

Ah. Didn't want Kellan to meet his mum, then. Which—obviously. And why would Kellan want that, anyway?

"Something tells me your mum wouldn't like my home address," he said casually.

"Something tells me it's none of my mom's business." Sam motioned to Winnie. "Or yours."

Kellan took his boxed treat and his loaf of bread in one hand and clapped Sam on the shoulder with the other. "I called him for landlord business."

"Right, I'm just here to check the kitchen sink," Sam said. "You said it was plugged?"

"Solid," Kellan replied, as if he'd not dealt with a thousand plugged sinks over the course of his career, and as if Winnie wouldn't know that from running her own food establishment and therefore read through Sam's lie in three seconds.

"The kitchen sink, huh? Is that what you kids are calling it these days?" Winnie shook her head and handed over two chocolate chip cookies in a small paper bag. "On the house. So long as you tell me how the French toast turns out."

Chapter Eight

"What's this about French toast?" Sam asked, waiting for Kell to unlock the door. It was weird standing on his own porch, hand pressed against the pink shingle siding, waiting for someone else to invite him into his own apartment.

"Winnie's jumping to conclusions, I think." *Tink*.

Sam was starting to realize Kell lost his *h*'s when he was nervous.

And Sam didn't mind the thought of putting him in that state. With all Kell's dreams and plans, he'd earn his own accolades one day, not just work under an executive chef with a world-class reputation. But today, Sam was in Kell's head, shaking up his thoughts, stealing letters from his lips.

A guy could get used to having that kind of effect on a person for longer than a month.

He shouldn't.

Couldn't. He wasn't suited to long-term anything.

And yet, he could not talk himself out of following Kell wherever the man wanted to take them.

"I might have jumped to some of the same conclusions as Winnie," Sam said.

The lock clicked open and Kell swung the door wide.

Sam entered the space, curious to see what Kell had done to it for his month in residence. Sam kept the rental fairly bare bones from a decor perspective, and he didn't often get to see what it looked like while occupied by a renter.

It was like doing one of those find-the-differences activities from kids' magazines that you browsed through when there was nothing to read at the dentist. The most obvious additions were the row of potted herbs along the windowsill and the neatly tied knife roll on the counter next to the fridge. A flash of deep blue caught his eye over one of the bistro-height chairs—a snuggly sweater of some kind. And a bookmarked paperback and a pair of horn-rimmed glasses perched on the end table next to Sam's favorite armchair.

He missed sitting in that chair. Hell, hopefully one day in the not-too-distant future, his dad would regain his equilibrium—emotional and physical—and Sam could move back in here, falling asleep to the sound of the boats creaking against the dock in the harbor and waking up to the sun on the water.

Kell cleared his throat, rubbing the back of his

neck and peering at Sam. "All's well? I've not ruined the place?"

"You're a model renter."

Lips—ones Sam would rather be kissing—twisted.
"You miss living here, don't you?"

"I do," he admitted.

"Got a timeline for moving back in, or is the change
permanent?"

"Hopefully the former, for my sake and my dad's.
He doesn't like his compromised independence any
more than I like seeing him unhappy. But we're
not there yet, especially not while the plumbing's
hooped." He scowled briefly. "We can't afford much
home care, and his hip injury hasn't healed enough
for him to shower unattended. Makes it tricky, especially in the evenings and overnight. It made more
sense for me to turn this place into a revenue stream
for the time being rather than driving back and forth
all the time."

"Probably makes French toast tricky, too."

"Often." Which meant expediency in the moments
he could carve away.

Kell set his bakery goodies on the island.

Sam shot a pointed look at the box and bread.
"How hungry are you? I have about an hour…" He
groaned. "Feels crappy to only be able to give short
chunks of time."

Kell stepped into Sam's space. Warm fingers slid
up his cheek, teasing the hair by his ear. "I'd hoped
to entice you to stay. But an hour's not noth—"

Sam dipped his head and stole the end of the sentence off Kell's mouth with a soft kiss. Heat filtered through his regret over how little he had to give, spreading through his limbs and settling in long-neglected places of his body.

Places begging him to take whatever it was Kell had to offer, however abbreviated.

"You're right. An hour isn't nothing." Or an hour and a half if he picked up fish and chips from Something's Fishy instead of barbecuing the chicken in the fridge. Take out would mean boiling less water for dishes, anyway, and—

"Hey. I lost you." Kell's lips teased his cheek. "Where'd you go?"

"Nowhere enjoyable."

"Appears I need to do a better job of keeping your attention."

"Or I need to get out of my head. I don't know why I'm drifting. I have this gorgeous man in front of me, and I'm thinking about—"

"About..." Kell prodded.

Chores? I'm awful. He shook his head.

"I'll tell you what I see." Warmth spread from Sam's cheek to his jaw as Kell drifted kisses in a soft line. "I see a man—and I'm not sure about using gorgeous for me, but it definitely applies to you—who's always up to ninety. He's keeping a lot of balls in the air. Important ones. Delicate, like those witch's balls they sell at the souvenir shop next to his mum's bakery. And he's so focused on not letting them fall and shatter, not letting down the people whom he loves, that it's hard to shift focus to something else."

Sam's breath caught. Most people assumed he was fine, but Kell saw the details. That meant more than Sam had realized it would. "Thank you."

"For what?"

"For understanding, I guess."

Kell's lips were feather light on Sam's cheek. "I want to help."

"You're already helping by not walking away when you catch me thinking about the dishes."

"Dishes." Kell guffawed, dropping his forehead briefly to Sam's shoulder. "Well, I've been guilty of that, too, especially when the hot water's shut off. Like I said—lots of balls. All sorts of colors flying through the air. You should try passing a few to other people now and again."

"I probably should." Sam stroked a hand down the wall of chest covered in soft cable-knit wool. A simple touch, but he could do it for hours. Heat twined through his core. He was itching for more, impatient, but also nervous. It had been a while since he did this with anyone he cared about. He shouldn't let himself care.

It's okay. Caring isn't love. When Kell left, it wouldn't be another round of watching the person he loved board the ferry, never to return. It wouldn't hurt.

"*Sam.*" An insistent mouth landed on his. Kell speared his fingers through Sam's hair and tugged, just enough to set Sam's nerve endings on fire. "Tell your mind to whisht. The dishes, the chores, all that responsibility that's weighing you down? That doesn't exist in this space. Not right now, anyway."

"Yeah? And then what?" Sam twined his fingers through Kell's.

"Endless possibilities. You could show me which of the arse grooves on the couch belong to you, and which of the Netflix recommendations are because of you or because of your guests."

Sam's heart sank. "You want to watch TV?"

"No, I've a yen to make you gasp and sigh and all manner of things." Talented fingers made quick work of the zipper on Sam's jacket. The material fell to the floor. "But I didn't want to assume you were in the mood for that."

Well, if they were going to shed outer layers... Sam slipped his hands under the bottom of the sexy cable knit that conjured images of cozy nights under a pile of blankets in an Irish cottage, warmed by a peat fire. Or maybe that was Scotland—

—not the point right now—

Focus. Bare skin under my fingertips.

He traced his thumbs along the hair-dusted planes of Kell's stomach. He'd tried so hard to ignore it while getting into and out of their wet suits, and now he didn't have to. "You're worried I'm not in the mood for this? My hint in the parking lot about warming up in the shower wasn't clear enough?"

Kell chuckled and nipped Sam's earlobe. "Another thing about which I didn't want to make assumptions."

The teeth rasping against tender flesh pulled a groan from his chest. "Assume away."

"Thing is, I'm already more than warm. Could probably skip the shower."

"Me, too," Sam said.

"Grand."

A quick zip, and Sam's thin hoodie was on the hardwood alongside his rain shell, leaving him in his T-shirt. A breeze blew through the cracked-open kitchen window, and the hair rose on his exposed forearms.

Kell ran his hands from Sam's biceps to his wrists. Another wave of goosebumps, for an entirely different reason.

Wouldn't be right to be the only person feeling that. Tugging Kell over to the couch, he said, "It's good for more than watching Netflix."

That got him a small smile, but the impact of it was like a cannonball. Damn, this man was potent.

"I was hoping," Kell said.

They landed on the soft seat, with Sam against a side cushion, legs tangled with Kell's. Why was being pinned down by a hot, eager body so blissful? Added to roaming hands and lips, to feeling Kell react to being over him, it took all of three seconds for Sam to start getting hard. The cinnamon aroma from the bakery clung to Kell's hair, mixing with an herbal soap smell on his skin. Damn, Sam wanted to lick that skin.

Kell shifted, somehow getting even closer than before. His leg pressed between Sam's thighs.

"*Christ.*" So much for being half stiff—there was no holding back with all that perfect weight against his lap.

Stroking a hand along his face, Kell tilted Sam's

cheek, piercing him with a questioning gaze. "Good blasphemy, or bad?"

He answered with a touch, gripping Kell's hips and rolling onto his side, taking advantage of the wide cushions. "Knew I bought the oversize couch for a reason."

Brushing a curl off Kell's forehead, something in Sam's stomach teetered, like he was falling further into whatever this was. This guy had him in thrall.

Irreparably? Maybe.

Caution...ease off... But he couldn't.

Denim rasped as he nudged a knee between Kell's, grinding a hip against muscle and aroused flesh.

The clock on the microwave glared at him, reminding him not to get too comfortable, but what was he supposed to do other than take everything Kell had to offer and hope he didn't get scowled at too fiercely when he finally peeled himself away and rolled in late with dinner?

"Show me what you like," Kell said.

"Just touch me. Wherever." Sam took the offered hand and laid it flat on his chest, right over his racing pulse. Slowly, he guided their palms over his pecs. "Have I mentioned how glad I am you showed up in my store?"

Kell flicked open the button on Sam's jeans. "Best web search result my sister ever got."

"I'll have to send the algorithm a thank-you card." Sam trailed his lips along the corded muscles in Kell's neck.

They kissed until it was hard for Sam to breathe or

think or do anything other than run his hands under that sweater that shouldn't have been so flattering.

His palms skimmed the skin above Kell's waistband, pushing the knit material higher. "This sweater's more Irish fisherman than London chef."

"I'm a bit of both."

"Well, it's hot. I love it." Sam lifted the hem and stripped it off, exposing Kell's stomach and chest. "I love it even better on the floor."

Kell let out a bark of laughter that was almost a moan. Gripping Sam's shoulders, he rolled onto his back and let his knees fall to either side, bringing Sam with him.

Sam settled into the V, stifling a groan of pleasure as his length met Kell's, teased and tempered by the layers of fabric still between them. It could not feel better than this.

Well, it could. Orgasms felt better.

In a different way, though.

There was something to be said for the anticipation. The edge between torment and tantalizing, the luxury of the build, the pressure, the need.

Of just being close to another person and blending together for a while, losing definition and forgetting all the details in the heat and comfort of someone else's arms.

Especially when that person tasted as good as Kellan Murphy.

His mouth reminded Sam of apples, kinda sweet, kinda tart, entirely delicious. He wanted more of it, of every part of Kell. With him, Sam felt calm, soothed. Needy sexually, but not emotionally.

"I feel so jagged around the edges by the end of the day. But you...you smooth them out," Sam whispered. "Being close to you, that is."

And he only wanted to be closer.

"We can get closer still." The accented words came on a strained breath, brushing Sam's ear. "If you care to."

"What, you're reading my mind now?" Sam said. "Stealing my thoughts?"

And my heart.

"Better if we don't think, like." Kell's fingers went back to the fly of Sam's jeans, teasing the zipper open. A knuckle brushed Sam's erection through his boxers.

His body tensed. Blood roared in his ears, the thrumming pulse almost a knocking sound.

Or—*damn it.*

Kell rose on an elbow and stared at the front entrance, a look of confusion where a moment before there had been only lust. "What the..."

Sam got off the couch so that Kell could get up. Snagging his sweater off the floor, Kell strode to answer, scowling as the sound got louder.

He was still putting his arms in his sleeves as he flung open the door.

Charlotte stood on the other side. Her gaze latched onto Kell's bare stomach for a brief second before he straightened his sweater.

"Winnie figured Sam might be here," she said.

And here Sam thought Winnie was trying to *en-*

courage his time alone with Kell. "You found me. Not that I was hiding."

But had I known, I might have. His neck prickled, and he rubbed it. He wasn't going to invite his sister in, because it wasn't technically his home. Kell took a few steps backward, mouth a bit agape, disappointment sharp on his features. He looked from Sam to Charlotte and back again.

"Sorry," Sam said to him.

"Why are you apologizing?" Charlotte cut in. "It's *your* apartment, and I'm your sister."

Rubbing wasn't doing the job of ridding his neck of its sudden stiffness. He started kneading. "It's Kell's for the month, Charlotte. What do you need?"

Her glare shifted from Kell to Sam. Specifically his pants, which, *damn it*, he'd forgotten to button up. He scrambled to fix his fly.

"Can I get a ride home? I finished more math tutoring with Nic, and it's raining so I didn't want to walk."

She had to be kidding. It was all of fifteen minutes if she cut through the baseball diamond. But Sam wasn't going to send her off at this point—the mood was annihilated beyond repair.

He grabbed his hoodie and jacket off the floor and held it casually in front of his crotch to spare his sister the reminder of what she'd walked in on. With her in the doorway, his reaction to Kell was fading fast, but it wasn't immediate, not with how much he'd wanted whatever they would have decided to do next. He glanced at the clock on the microwave. So much for his full hour of time to himself.

He brushed a thumb along Kell's cheekbone and tried to fill his gaze with as much promise as he was capable of. "Meet me at the dock in the morning for a paddle. On the house. We'll go out for an hour before I open the shop."

Kell's arms were crossed over his chest, and his expression was impassive. "Sure. Half eight?"

"Can't wait." Sam left, following his sister, who at least had the grace to look sheepish.

Irritation burned during their whole walk to the truck, still parked in his angled spot outside Otter Marine Tours.

"I didn't know I'd be interrupting," she said petulantly. That "I know I screwed up, but I don't want to admit it" tone that teenagers were good at. He knew it well, and had been a master of it himself in high school.

"You couldn't have guessed?" he said.

"I'm not used to you dating anyone."

"Yeah, well, get used to it, okay? I'm not planning on being a monk for the rest of my life. It's been long enough since my divorce—I'm ready to see people again."

"Okay," Charlotte said, voice sad. She paused for a long moment, getting in the passenger seat and slamming the door. Staring at her fingernails, she picked at a chip in her lime-green nail polish. "I always kind of hoped Alyssa would come home. You're sure she won't?"

"A hundred percent." Their divorce papers were long ago filed. His ex was living in Seattle with her new boyfriend and three cats and was running a successful nail salon.

"She made time for me. Mom doesn't." Her throat bobbed. "I see *your* mom more than I see mine."

Oh. Damn. He put an arm around his sister. "I'm sorry, Charlie."

Sorry he'd screwed up his marriage, sorry he couldn't fill that hole.

But even if he should be, he wasn't sorry he'd tried to take an hour to have a good time with a sexy, willing man.

Kellan leaned against the boardwalk rail at a quarter past eight the next day, waiting for Sam. For once, the ocean was dead calm. The sun was rising over the mountains on the horizon. Crisp white peaks scraped the sky in the distance; lower, rounded islands jostled for space up close. The previous day's rain was all but a memory.

The annoyance over the interruption was not.

He understood what it was like dealing with teenage sisters, not that Aoife had been one for over a decade. He also understood how dealing with major life changes could narrow a person's perspective, and he got the sense Charlotte was going through that. Hell, he'd done it himself, burning out at work in the wake of losing Aoife. Sam's sister barreling in with a selfish request, interrupting Sam's time, was child's play.

Kellan didn't have to like it, though. He craved time alone with Sam outside of work hours. They'd been on the verge of some sort of pleasure yesterday, and nothing Kellan managed alone in bed last night came close to being pinned to the couch by a burly, soft-hearted divemaster.

He needed to talk to someone, but it wasn't the kind of thing he felt like sharing with Rory, who, despite being married and in love, tended to be cynical about relationships. Nor was he about to call up his therapist for dating advice. It wasn't anxiety related; he didn't need to pay someone to listen to him complain about wanting sex.

So he was stuck with an envelope, hoping for some sort of wisdom in his sister's script. He should have opened it days ago, but the longer he left it, the harder it was to open. What if this was the final letter? She might have finished this one and then felt too sick to write more. There was no guarantee one would be waiting for him in his hotel in Okinawa.

Hand shaking, he ripped open the seam and took out the sheet of letterhead.

His heart sank when he saw how few words marked the page. He read slowly, trying to soak up every vowel and consonant.

My favourite gobshite—
You're both those things, you know.
    It's killing me not to know if you've made it this far.
    No wait, that's cancer.
    Sweet Jesus, I love you. Carry that with you, okay?
—A

It wasn't enough. It would never be enough. His chest burned, a storm of unshed tears and endless lamentation. He bloody hated these letters.

Folding it with shaking hands, he tucked it in his pocket and wiped hot streaks from his cheeks with the back of his hand.

Mother of God, he needed to get ahold of himself before Sam got here.

Pressing the heels of his hands into his eyelids, he took a four-second breath in and let an eight-second breath out.

A door opened and closed and then footsteps approached from behind him. Sturdy hands gripped his shoulders, a touchpoint to something alive and hearty.

He swallowed a sob.

"The immeasurable price we pay for loving people," Sam murmured.

"I'd pay it e-every time."

Steely arms banded around him, pulling him back to front, into a cloak of warmth. A light breeze brushed his face, but the cold didn't sink in, not while he was surrounded by Sam's heat and care.

He matched his breathing to the rhythm of the water lapping the rocks below until the cramps between his ribs finally released. "Okay. I think I'm okay."

"To go out on the water? Are you sure? We could get a coffee instead."

"No, I need to do these things." *Even if Aoife can't see me.*

He turned, not bothering to put on a smile.

Earnest eyes gave him the once-over. "You'll be warm enough in that, but not if you fall in. I was thinking you could try a dry suit. They're best for paddle-boarding."

"For what?" His heart rate jumped. "I thought we'd be kayaking."

Concern tugged at Sam's mouth. The early sun caught the lighter copper strands in his hair. "We could, but the tide's just right for stand-up paddling this morning. It's slack, so we'll be able to get around the point into the next bay without getting pulled into the ferry's path. It's rarely this calm in March. We should take advantage. Kayaking's awesome, but SUP is even more special."

The prospect of floating on top of the water with only four inches of fiberglass and epoxy between him and the deep, dark depths was…he wasn't right sure. Sam had shown him enough incredible things that curiosity pricked at him. The next bay could be marvelous.

And Aoife's letter had left him as sore as a pair of road-rashed knees, but maybe that would work in his favor. He was all emotioned out for the morning.

"Lead the way to the dry suits," he said.

Once inside, he took off his jacket and started to remove his long-sleeved technical shirt.

"You can leave that on," Sam said. "Your sweat-pants are thin enough, too."

Kellan winked at him. "You sound disappointed."

"I am. Slept like garbage last night, thinking of you."

Never before had someone's rough sleep made him feel so chuffed.

"I tell you what. I will be exceedingly brave today and won't complain a bit about you putting me in mortal peril. And in exchange, you will talk to whomever you need to talk to and arrange for a whole night off in the near future, on one of those few days of home care you mentioned your dad having. No demands for rides, no requests for homework, no rescues from the pub. So long as someone's helping your dad, the rest of them can solve their own problems for a few hours."

Blinking, Sam froze with a dry suit half off the hanger.

Damn. Had Kellan jammed his nose in where it didn't belong?

In for a penny...

"It's okay that they need you," he continued. "Especially when you're dealing with health needs. But there's a fine line between helping and being taken advantage of."

Sam looked stricken for a long moment.

The sound of a key in the lock of the front door startled them both.

Kellan was left with the rotting feeling in his gut that he'd spoken out of turn.

Sam's young employee—Nic, if Kellan remembered rightly—came through the front door with Charlotte tucked under his arm. Their heads were together, and they were laughing in that secretive way couples shared.

Sam stiffened.

The pair froze. Nic lost five shades of color from his tawny-brown cheeks.

"Uh, Sam—I forgot my hiking shoes here in the back room last night. Needed them because Charlotte and I are going to jog up Teapot Hill."

"You're scheduled today," Sam said tersely. "For one o'clock."

Nic nodded eagerly. "I know. We'll be back by then."

Kellan reached out and rubbed Sam's biceps, trying to soothe away some of his tension. Didn't work. The muscle was a rock under his palm.

"Be careful," Sam said to his sister.

Charlotte snuggled closer to her friend, if that was even possible. "Uh, hypocrite much?"

"Charlotte," Nic said quietly, disentangling himself. "Easy." He hurried into the back room, returning quickly with his shoes.

Chestnut brows lifted nearly to Sam's hairline. He blinked at his sister. "I meant be safe while *hiking.*"

"Yeah, right. You meant you're allowed to have fun and I'm not." She grabbed her boyfriend's hand. "Let's go, Snickers."

Snickers. Poor Sam.

"Want me to lock up on my way out?" Sam's employee said over his shoulder, a mix of apology and nervousness in his eyes.

"I've got it," Sam said. "And really, be safe. All this rain—parts of that trail get loose."

"Don't worry, boss," Nic said. "We'll see you in a couple of hours."

The door clicked behind the pair.

Groaning, Sam went to lock it. "I swear I was changing her diapers and giving her a bottle yesterday. When did she get old enough to call boys 'Snickers' in one breath and be a smartass in the next?"

"Having gotten stupid over a boy a number of times myself when I was her age, I'd say it probably happened in the last couple years."

"At some point I wasn't looking."

"If fooling around with me is causing irreparable damage, I can back off," Kellan said, even though he hated every word of it.

"Absolutely not. *And* I'm going to take your advice, make myself unavailable for a night." Sam's smile turned sly. "To everyone except you, anyway."

Sam's declaration was still slapping around in Kellan's head twenty minutes later, lapping at his focus like the ripples against his paddleboard. It was nice to be prioritized, made to feel important.

Gave him something to think about instead of being on the water, too. He was bone dry in the neck-to-ankles suit—his feet, even, with boots—but cold still seeped in somehow. "Something tells me this will be warmer in Australia."

"A balmy forty-five degrees isn't working for you?" Sam teased, leading the way with easy paddle strokes toward the point of treed rock. They were headed out of the harbor in the opposite direction from where they'd gone out in Sam's boat. "I would have thought with your Irish roots you'd be used to a chilly sea."

He cut his paddle into the water and followed his guide. "My sister and I spent summers with our gran, and she lived a stone's throw from the water. I used to be impervious to the cold. Apparently, I've become more used to my creature comforts." He frowned. "I wonder sometimes…"

Sam turned his head, quiet question on his face.

"This list Aoife gave me—I wonder if it was less about her unfinished dreams and more about genuinely wanting an adventure for me."

Sam slowed, only picking up his pace again when Kellan's board was in line with his own. "I bet it's frustrating not to be able to ask."

The water lapping over the tip of his paddleboard mirrored the grief sloshing in his stomach. "To say the least."

"I'm sorry, I don't know what to say. I've never lost anyone like you have with your sister."

"Grief doesn't have to be about death, Sam. You're helping your dad grieve whatever life it was that he had before his accident." He didn't have all the details, but the Walker family was obviously dealing with deep wounds.

Gripping his paddle horizontally, Sam glided across the calm water. Kellan stopped stroking, too, waiting for Sam to process whatever was causing him to stare off into the distance.

"Franci was driving them home from the garden store. She does all the gardening at my dad's place.

Because she likes it and doesn't have much yard access in the basement suite she rents," Sam explained. "You should talk vegetables with her one day. She geeks out on beets like no one's business."

"Beets are worthy of geekery," Kellan said.

Sam smiled sadly. "Now there's a rabbit trail."

"Sure, you're allowed to veer off topic."

"The story isn't much fun to listen to." He blew out a breath. "They got T-boned at the intersection in front of the elementary school. Some of the plants flew over the fence and landed in the playground. Like, literally on the equipment. I noticed that, first. Little sprouts of green and clumps of brown splattered on the yellow slide. An off-duty police officer, a woman from my grad class, came into the store and told me what happened. I ran the three blocks to the accident site. Why I fixated on the plants instead of the truck on its side or the helicopter landing in the field to airlift my dad, I don't know."

With careful side strokes, Kellan brought his board close enough to Sam's to be able to reach over and put his hand on the other man's shoulder. "Little things stick out sometimes. Did Franci get airlifted, too?"

"No. She went by ambulance—well, and the ferry—to the hospital on San Juan Island. She wasn't injured as badly."

Kellan's board wobbled with a small wave, and he gripped Sam tighter.

Sam stiffened just as a second wave hit. Their boards knocked together. Kellan let go to put his arms out for balance, instinctively bending his knees and dropping his paddle. He pitched back and forth, and his stomach lurched.

A sharp curse came from his left, followed by a splash that echoed off the shore.

Kellan knelt on his board to fully regain his balance and took in the empty board floating a few feet away. Sam bobbed in the water, his thin, knit cap bright against the shiny jade-black surface. His hands were busy below the surface, no doubt removing the Velcro strap tethering the board to his ankle.

"Sweet Jesus, I didn't push you in, did I?" he asked Sam.

"No, that was my fault."

It wasn't hard to see why the man was a professional. The powerful swimming strokes, the efficient retrieval of both paddles—he was fluid, beautiful to watch. So easy and relaxed in the water despite them being a ways off shore and unable to see the bottom.

The urge came out of nowhere, but Kellan wanted to surprise his teacher more than he wanted to avoid the deep. Taking a ragged breath and balancing his newly returned paddle on the deck of the board, he slid into the ocean.

Cold slapped his chin and cheeks, but not the rest of him. What an odd sensation, being submerged and completely dry. The water pressed his thermal layer and suit to his body.

Sam let out a hoot of laughter. "If you can't beat 'em, join 'em?"

"Something like that." Kellan wiped salt water from his eyes with a gloved thumb. "More that you made it look easy, and I figured I could give it a lash. What are we in, a hundred feet of water?"

"More like two."

"Oof, way to make a fella feel better."

Three gliding strokes and Sam was at his side, treading water. He offered both hands to Kellan. "I'm here if you need me."

It was a nice offer, but happily, unnecessary. So long as he was the subject of Sam's whole focus, there was no space to worry about a little ocean depth.

"Impressive egg-beater technique. The lifeguard of my dreams," Kellan teased.

The man of my dreams, even.

Wasn't that just an impossibility?

"I might have a lifesaving course or two under my belt," Sam said, returning his hands to the water and pulling Kellan's board over to them. He kept a hand on the edge. Kellan followed suit. The support meant not having to kick so hard, being able to float. Right close to Sam.

Probably gazing in a lovesick manner, but good God, his instructor's face begged for attention.

And his mouth begged to be kissed.

Unable to resist, Kellan leaned in. Under the salt of the ocean, Sam tasted like minty toothpaste, a hint of coffee. The flavors of a day just starting. Kellan could see waking up to Sam's lips on his. Him, sleeping in after a late night at the restaurant. Sam, up early to take a tour group out in the zodiac, giving Kellan something to think about for the rest of the morning.

Only problem being, he was building a restaurant halfway around the world from the zodiac. They wouldn't ever be in the same place for good-morning kisses.

The wake of a boat broke them apart, and they rose and fell in tandem.

Kellan hoisted himself back onto his board.

Sam followed suit and regained his balance in the blink of an eye. "Still dry? Seals holding? Not too cold?"

"Doing fine."

"What about meeting me after work and taking the boat out to one of the dive sites? If you can swim here, you can swim there, no problem."

And maybe they'd get some of that evening time alone Sam had promised. Kellan shot him a thumbs-up. "You're on."

Chapter Nine

"Not your usual seagoing fare," Archer said, stealing a cracker from the picnic Sam had thrown together in a rushed trip to the grocery store during his lunch break.

His employee crunched on the seedy round before grabbing another handful and tossing them into his mouth one by one.

"Hey," Sam protested. "Those are for my tour. Er, swim. I'm taking Kell out to the point to practice."

"So, a date?" Archer smirked, pointing at the cooler of food.

At least he couldn't see the contents of the duffel bag, too—he'd no doubt give Sam the gears over the blankets and pillow tucked inside.

It was going to be a clear night. Perfect for the stargazing Sam had mentioned to Kell. And with his dad occupied with his home care nurse and Charlotte and

Franci under strict orders *not* to call unless the house was burning down, tonight was Sam's best chance to prove he hadn't been exaggerating about the view of far-off galaxies.

So yeah—a date.

"Guess you could call it that," he conceded.

"Right on," Archer said. "Thought I caught him looking at you that way."

Sam shrugged but was warmed by the thought. It felt good to catch someone's eye, even when it was temporary. Especially when it was temporary. He wasn't going to repeat the mistake of getting attached to someone who'd end up leaving him.

"So I shouldn't send out the Coast Guard if you aren't in by nine?" Archer asked around his final mouthful.

"You better not."

"With how badly you need to get laid? I won't."

Sam shot him a middle finger.

Archer snorted. "Tell Charlotte to call me if she needs something."

"Thanks. Really."

He shot that off in a text to his sister and finished prepping the equipment and packing the gear to the boat. The same suits he and Kell had worn earlier in the day, the food and duffel, towels, his nagging libido...

Ordering the need to jump Kell's bones to calm down for now, he sat down on the center block seat to make sure he had everything.

He and Archer had made a thousand jokes about

using the wide, backless bench as a bed. And maybe his friend had tried it out at some point, but Sam hadn't.

Lying back with one knee bent and foot propped on the cushioned surface, he shifted around, testing his weight, until he heard footsteps approaching. He sat, grinning at his guest making his way down the ramp.

Kell came to a halt next to the *Oyster Queen*, looking cozy in a thick hoodie and lounge pants. "Room on there for a tagalong?"

The question was gentle and musical, the sound of a thousand chilly nights spent cozying up by a fire, sipping whisky and making wild plans for the future. He suspected those things would be just as good in Ireland or London as they would here.

Guilt jolted him. What was he doing, wishing for something different when he knew it couldn't work?

He waved his guest aboard. "My boat is your boat."

Kell put a hand on the dockside gunwale and swung his leg over. After getting his footing, he dropped his backpack next to Sam's bags near the front. His eyes lit up when he saw the cooler.

"I figured it was my turn," Sam said, trying to sound matter of fact but for sure coming off too eager.

Kell's smile widened. "I'm like that loyal Labrador of Archer's, Sam. Feed me treats, and I'm your friend for life."

"It's nothing fancy."

"If it's something I didn't make, I'll love it."

Sam raised his eyebrows. "You seem to live for cooking, with how much food you've brought me."

"Cooking is grand. So is not cooking. You know how it is. When it's your job, even if you adore it, it still feels like a job." Kell jammed his hands in the pockets of his sweatshirt. "I'm sure taking me out on trips like this feels partly like work."

"I would have thought so, but..." The prospect of taking Kell swimming and then hanging on the boat promised nothing but a good time. "But teaching you is fun."

His honesty earned him another broad smile.

"Well, that's good news, because this is fun for me, too. Even though I prepped some treats of my own and have them in my backpack."

"You didn't have to," Sam said. "Don't ever feel obligated to bring food if it's a burden."

Quiet seriousness crossed Kell's face. "Nothing's a burden with you. If you're not careful, you'll never get rid of me."

Sam gripped the edge of the bench and forced a laugh, knowing the sentiment was a joke, but really, the idea of Kell being close by was damn fantastic. What would it be like to be in the grocery store and bump into that smile? Or get to take him out for boat rides on any old day, not because Kell wanted to pass his diving certification? Making those gray eyes light up was becoming an addiction for Sam.

Stop it. Alyssa stayed on the island for you and was miserable. Learn your lesson.

Couldn't ignore that logic. Sam deflated into the seat. This was about today and the next couple weeks, not about having the chef on Oyster Island in any permanent sense.

Kell pointed at the free-standing seat next to the captain's chair. "Best place for me, I assume?"

"If we're talking best places, I'd suggest this one." Sam stood and sidled in close, waiting a second to make sure Kell was good with the contact, with lips on his cheek and jaw, hands on his lean hips. The pants he wore were no doubt warm but thin enough Sam could feel muscle and definition that jeans disguised.

"I think you're right." Kell feathered soft kisses along his jaw, tiny sparks that Sam felt clear to his core.

Strong hands stroked his back. Sam let himself fall into the kiss. It snuck up on him like a wave, stronger than he expected, sudden, disorienting.

Tossing him head over feet, swamping his reality.

Warm and hungry lips devoured Sam's, coaxing and greedy with every nip.

Kissing Kell was a release from reality, something Sam hadn't felt in so long. He and his ex-wife had lost this early in their relationship. How had he lived without it since? His hands couldn't be in enough places at once, wanting to explore every inch of Kell.

An eagle's caw broke through the insular cocoon they'd so quickly woven.

Kell leaned back, scanning the sky for the bird. "Bastard sounds close."

"More eagles than people on the island," Sam said, taking a step back and wiping a hand down his face. "They keep their distance, though."

The powerful six-foot wingspan whooshed as the bird glided past and then landed on one of the pilings at the end of the dock.

"Incredible." Awe tinged Kell's voice. "I could watch it for hours." He brushed a thumb down Sam's cheek. "Though, right now, I'd rather look at you."

"Sweet talker."

"I'll own that."

They didn't talk much on the ten-minute trip to the south point of the island, where the currents and a rock face made for some spectacular dive conditions. He knew Kell would be hooked the minute he got forty feet down and turned on a light for the first time, supplying the beam needed to see the full spectrum of reds, oranges and yellows, the wavelengths of which the ocean absorbed the deeper a diver swam. Sam also knew that fear was nothing to play with, and that not everyone could overcome it to get that far down. His failure rate as an instructor was low, but there were still some, and he respected that. The sport was usually safe, but it wasn't for everyone.

That said, he loved sharing it with the people he cared about. Archer, Matias, his sisters… Some of his favorite memories were when he took them somewhere and showed them something incredible.

He used to share it with his dad, too.

He gripped the steering wheel. That wouldn't be happening any time soon, if ever. People with mobility issues could dive—Archer, with his above-the-knee prosthesis, was proof of that—but his dad had shown no interest in going underwater since his accident.

"Hey." Kell rose from his chair and moved to stand behind Sam. The casual loop of his arms, fingers lazily stroking the open V at Sam's neck, sent a shiver up Sam's spine. "Why the frown?"

"Sorry. Started thinking about my dad. He taught me how to dive. We used to take trips together whenever we could, for his spring break or during the summer or both. We'd spend more time underwater than above."

"Don't tell me you broke the safety guidelines for how long you can stay submerged." The teasing words brushed past Sam's ear with a swirl of air.

"Never. I had a friend get the bends once, flying in a small plane too soon after diving. It's no joke." He tipped his head and sneaked a kiss on the underside of Kell's jaw, loving Kell's quiet gasp. "I maximize my surface intervals to the minute, though. If you're going to fly halfway around the world, you gotta spend every minute you can checking out the local scenery. I hope you're able to once you're on the next leg of your journey."

"That's the plan." Kell kissed his temple, his ear. Sam swallowed a groan, trying not to let his body react. "Though I've got so much more to do here before I leave."

Me. Please let "more to do" be me. Blood roared in Sam's ears, echoing the growl of the engine. Rounding one last point, he pulled back on the throttle and eased the boat in place. "Here we are."

Kell drew back, crossed his arms and stared at the cliff face, jagged and imposing above still, slack water. "Let's do this."

Sam hooked up to a buoy he'd fixed long ago, proud of Kell's persistence.

They got their suits on, complete with hoods, boots and gloves.

"You can wear your fins and mask or leave them off. Whatever makes you most comfortable."

"Best to start how I'll go on. I'll wear them and see how it goes."

Sam stepped off the platform first. The cold immediately chilled his lips and the exposed skin around his mouth. He treaded water and looked up at Kell, who stood on the edge of the platform, mouth pressed in a tight line. His mask made it hard to read his expression, but Sam imagined there was a fair amount of white rimming the gray irises.

"You okay?" Sam asked. "Take your time. I can float here for hours."

"Braggart," Kell said lightly.

"Or an unapologetic exaggerator."

Kell's chest rose and fell. His snorkel, attached to the strap of his mask, dangled unused beside his cheek. "No promises for how long I'll last, but here goes nothing." He executed a textbook giant stride entry and shot Sam an *okay* hand signal a second after surfacing.

"Beauty." Sam swam backward for ten feet, getting them away from the boat.

Kell followed, lip sandwiched between his teeth, making his cheeks balloon out with each breath.

Not the most relaxed Sam had ever seen him, but better than when they'd started their lessons.

"Scale of one to ten, how much do you want to climb back onto the boat right now?" Sam asked, partly to get a gauge of Kell's nerves, partly to get him to stop biting his lip so he could breathe easier.

"A four?" Kell's voice squeaked.

"The minute you're done, you call it." He swam closer to be in reach, just in case.

"I'm sorry. This is so boring for you," Kell said, rising on a small wave and keeping himself afloat with careful strokes.

"Not at all. And besides, I've been down there so many times, I could draw you a map from memory." He crooked a finger at his student. "Let's try something."

Kell closed the last few feet of distance between them, curiosity brightening his gaze.

"Float with me," Sam said. "Let me set the scene for you."

Sam indicated for Kell to take his hand and then splayed out on his back on the surface with their fingers entwined together.

Kell relaxed into a floating position. "You've got me rafting like an otter."

"Otters know what's going on."

"I saw one swimming off the dock the other morning. I was on your balcony. Made for excellent viewing with my coffee and croissant."

"I'm sad I missed that."

"The otter?" Kell said. "You've probably seen a million of them."

"Not with you, though. And not while enjoying coffee and breakfast."

"Something else to plan for?" So much hope threaded Kell's words, enough to make Sam feel like he could float five inches above the water, let alone on the surface.

"Yes, please," Sam said.

"That probably wasn't the scene you were planning to set, though," Kell said.

"Not exactly, but I think I like it better."

Kell squeezed his hand. "Me too."

Sam cleared his throat. "Nine feet under, there's a shelf with enough plumed anemones on it that you'll think they're taking over the world. Around seventeen feet, it's urchins. At thirty-two, it's worth turning on a flashlight—there's a section of coralline algae that's pinker than anything you've seen in your life. And at forty-four, if we're lucky, we'll see a pair of wolf eels."

"Wolf eels." Kell's tone was cautious. "Aoife talked about seeing those. They're a subsection of her list."

"I'll do my best to help you check it off."

The waves lifted and settled them gently. Silence spanned, but it was never quiet. Waves smacked the cliff, a seagull complained about life to one of his buddies, the rumble of a boat engine carried across the water from a distance.

"Sam?"

"Yeah?"

"I don't care about the list at the moment. I'm not scared," Kell said. "But I'm done floating. Let's eat. And then see where the night takes us."

They got out of the water and back into their clothes in record time.

Scarfed down their picnic, too.

Sam checked his watch. "We have hours until we'll be able to stargaze."

Kell shot him a *whatever shall we do?* look. "Still worth getting comfortable to watch the sunset."

Sam gathered the blankets and tilted his head at the bow. "If you're up for skirting the wheelhouse, I can vouch for the view from the foredeck."

And it was. With the windshield angled at their backs, one blanket cushioning them from the wood decking and the other protecting them from the wind off the water, being absolutely alone—it was better than Sam had pictured.

Kell snuggled close, bringing the thick quilt around his back to fend off the early spring wind. His hand rested on Sam's chest. Holy crap, the smell of the sea on Kell's skin, mixing with whatever rosemary-scented shampoo or bodywash he used—Sam couldn't get enough of it. He took a deep breath, savoring the sensory overload.

If he wasn't careful, he'd topple mask over fins for this guy.

Keep it light, Walker.

"We'll have to keep each other warm if we're going to last long enough to see stars," Sam said.

"Bet I could have you seeing them before darkness sets." The words came with a cheeky grin.

"Promises." Sam leaned in and kissed it away, coaxing Kell's lips from teasing to serious. The moan that followed didn't hurt, either. Sam skimmed a hand along fleece. So many possibilities below the fabric. He tugged the zipper down, then dipped his fingers under the hem of the soft T-shirt he'd exposed.

Hair-dusted skin rasped his fingertips and he rolled onto a hip to bring their bodies front-to-front. Their breath mingled.

Kell skimmed his palms along Sam's back, chest, arms, like he was learning every angle. "This is about where we left off, is it not?"

"When my sister interrupted? I think you had on less clothes. And my fly had definitely been taken care of."

Firm hands cupped Sam's ass. "No need for that with your joggers."

"Right." He could feel everything more, too, through the layers of his sweatpants and Kell's. That unmistakable heightening of warmth that only bodies could create.

Pulling Sam tighter to his front, Kell shifted his hips. A breath shuddered from his lips, and he pushed at the waistband of Sam's sweats. "These will be much, much simpler than jeans." He served a mind-melting kiss. "Don't get me wrong—I do fancy your arse in denim. But ease of access can't be overstated."

Sam slid a hand around to Kell's front, cupping him, stroking him, hopefully making it damn clear that there was nowhere in the world he'd rather be right now than making out on the bow of his boat. Tugging on that plush lower lip with his teeth, he let himself slip further into the haze of need.

There was kissing and touching, and then there was kissing and touching Kellan Murphy, and he didn't want to put too much thought into how and why it felt special, distinctive.

The only thoughts worth having were about bringing this man pleasure and joining him for the ride. There was something about being with a person that was different when you knew there was no possible way you'd get interrupted. Sam wanted to speed up to get to the fireworks and slow down to savor the build all at the same time.

"What do you like?" he asked, embarrassingly close to panting from tasting Kell's mouth alone. "Fast? Slow? Touching? Penetration? Top? Bottom?"

Kell laughed. "I'm happy to fill out a checklist if you like."

"Sorry." Sam's cheeks burned. "That did sound like a multiple-choice test."

"I've a mind to choose 'all of the above.'" Kell kissed his way down Sam's neck, leaving behind a trail of heat. "Maybe not on a boat, though. Little complicated to deal with all the accessories."

"Oh, I don't know." He reached under Kell's waistband and underwear and caressed hot, hard skin. Yearning seared low in his belly. "A person could get creative with the captain's chair."

He could think of five ways to bend Kell over, or

to be the one bent. The seat, the back, hell, even the dashboard—

"I'm worried if I strip off your clothes here, they'll end up in the drink," Kell said.

"I'm willing to take that risk. Or we kiss for now and save the clothes removal for later."

Please don't choose door number two. Sam was hot and antsy and looking for ways to get closer. Yeah, he had his hand down Kell's pants, was setting a slow, testing rhythm. But it wasn't enough. His own erection was begging for attention, teased by being cupped through cotton and rubbing against another arousal.

"We're not just kissing, Sam." An impatient but amused correction. "You all set on the health front?"

"Yeah."

"Me, too." Kell hooked his thumbs into Sam's sweats and underwear and shoved them past his butt. He sprang free. Relief, not being constrained. Unsatisfied, needing pressure, needing more, needing skin on skin. He pushed Kell's pants down, too. Before he could do anything else, a hungry mouth settled on his, a hand tangled in the back of his hair. Kell took them both in hand.

The confident grip commanded Sam's hungry body. So good. Gently thrusting his hips in rhythm with the strokes, he buried his face into Kell's neck and swore.

"This what you want?"

Sam swore again. "It's just your hand. It shouldn't be this good."

Gentle lips teased his ear. "Sometimes you get lucky."

"I feel that. Feel lucky."

Along with all sorts of emotions he knew would only lead to pain. Sam could fool himself all he wanted, but this man wouldn't be easy to say goodbye to.

Another stroke, and Sam's control slipped. He dropped frenzied kisses along Kell's jaw, pressed closer with his hips and let himself ride the edge of release.

"I'm close," he said.

"So am I." The accented words were a harsh whisper. Kell's rhythm matched the power and pace of the ocean slapping the boat's hull. His fingers tightened around their lengths and he let out a gasp. "I can't..."

The gasp turned to a groan. Kell pressed his cheek to Sam's, his body rigid.

Sam couldn't have held back, even if he wanted to. Climax swept through him, ears roaring and vision flashing incandescent. He gripped Kell's shoulders and let himself go deep under, the plummet of a cliff dive followed by the sweet caress of water pulling him under, enveloping him and pressing him from all sides.

Leaving him with the hum of the rush, lungs heaving and pulse flying.

And still the man in his arms, a dazed expression on his face as he untangled his fingers from their lengths and took in a shuddery breath.

"I have Kleenex in my pocket," Sam said. Not that he had the strength to reach for it, but still.

"I couldn't move to get it, even if I wanted to," Kell said, looping his arms around Sam and holding him close.

Damn, it was reassuring not to be the only person thrown for a loop by an orgasm.

No, not just the orgasm. The intimacy of it. The growing suspicion that this, the cuddling after release, was what kept a person going through the hard times.

He let himself relax into Kell's comforting embrace. Time whiled away.

They eventually cleaned up and got straightened out, just as the sun was kissing the horizon, turning the sky into a rainbow of pastels and fading light.

Lying with his back against the windows, with Kell seamed to Sam's side and drawing lazy circles along his belly, Sam couldn't think of the last time he'd been able to totally disconnect from everything except the current moment.

"Thank you," he murmured. "For insisting we get away. I can actually hear my thoughts out here."

Which wasn't totally a good thing because there was a whole lot of his gut shouting at him that a couple of weeks with Kell wasn't going to be enough.

"That sunset makes me wonder why I don't prioritize watching one every night," Kell said.

"You get many sunsets on the water in London?"

Kell's gaze shifted. "On the Thames, when the weather's favorable. Not that I see many of them. Evening shifts."

Sam nodded, brushing a strand of hair away from the face he was dying to kiss again.

What's stopping me?

Who knew? He brushed his lips along sun-kissed skin. "Matias doesn't complain, but I see the strain of starting his shift when everyone else is done with their workday."

"Sure." Kell bit his lip. "I noticed it less when I was in the throes of running a kitchen. Sometimes when you're grieving, you see things in a way you've not before, like. I've slowed down here."

"Hazard of being on the island."

"Like I said before, I'm starting to wonder about Aoife's motives in sending me on this trip. I talked to my business partner this afternoon. He's still working for the restaurant I most recently quit—he'll be their pastry chef until we're ready with Aisling. He was nearing the end of his night and sounded so bloody tired."

"Any job has those moments, right?" Even Sam's— he dealt with irritating customers and the occasional diver breaking the rules, and had a low-income month now and again that kept him up at night.

"It does," Kell said cautiously. "And I don't mind the food-related stress. Striving for a perfect service is what makes it worth it."

"Having your own place will be a thrill, too."

"I thought so." Doubt rode the words, the same disconcerted edge Sam had heard the last time they'd talked about Kell's restaurant.

"But?" Sam said, tightening an arm around Kell's back.

"Are the accolades really worth the stress?"

Oof, tough question. "Wish I could answer that for you."

Kell barked out a laugh. "I wish you could, too. Once I've received Aoife's money, I'll have my dream at my fingertips. But lately, when I fall asleep at night, it's not a busy bistro that's on my mind."

"What is?"

"Lately?" Kell laughed again. "It's been getting you naked. You're distracting, Sam Walker."

His heart squeezed. "In a good way, I hope."

"Certainly."

"Not that I want to get in the way of your dream."

Gentle fingers twirled around Sam's navel. "When I'm on a tear, nothing turns my head unless it's something that deserves my attention."

Not having an easy reply, Sam kissed the top of the mussed, dark head.

"And usually," Kell continued, "if I let my head get turned, it's because I need to reevaluate how I'm directing my time."

"Hmm."

"I love cooking new food, trying new things, being on the edge."

"But?" Sam asked.

Kell chuckled. "Yes. *But*. Being here has reminded me how good it is to breathe. To play with food, explore new and exciting ideas. I've done that since I've arrived, and I've loved being inspired again. I'm worried that inspiration will die if I'm consumed with numbers and elbow rubbing and blog mentions that come with opening a new place."

"That's…that's big," Sam said.

"Sure." He grunted unhappily. "With Gran and Aoife gone, aside from a few friends, work was all I had left. Thought that was normal. Seeing you with your family reminded me it's not."

Sam's throat tightened. "There's no way my family makes being close look good."

"You do, though. Yes, you personally sacrifice a lot. Could probably find a better line between helping them and self-care. But you love each other, so much. For a bloke left wondering if his parents ever read the magazine articles he sends them when he's made the front cover, makes him realize what he's missing, like."

"Makes sense, I guess."

Kell paused for a slew of heartbeats. His breath shuddered out, long and raw. "I can think of my restaurant staff as my family all I want, but at the end of the night, they'd be going home to warm beds and a welcoming snog, and I'd be sitting there in my office, popping antacids and beta blockers."

"I… That's a crappy mental picture, Kellan."

"It is. Even the idea of putting something of Gran and Aoife into the place… I don't know. No matter how perfect I build it, it won't… It won't be the same as sharing a cuppa with them."

They lay snuggled in silence for a while. Sam could slowly feel the tension leaching from Kell's body. A rocking hull and dimming sunset had a way of doing that.

"I don't know what my life would look like if I

wasn't trying to climb to the top of the food world, though."

"I have a hard time picturing you anywhere but a kitchen." Sam chuckled. "Except maybe here. You fit nicely on my boat." Yikes, that was way too significant a statement. "Not forever," he corrected. "But in the here and now."

Kell hummed. Sam didn't know how to read the sound.

He cleared his throat. "You going to talk to your business partner about it?"

"I think I'll have to. Opening a restaurant takes everything from you, every ounce of your soul. And I'm not much feeling like giving up all of myself to the plan we've made."

"I hope you figure it out. For your sake."

With a gleam in his eye, Kell straddled Sam's hips. "Me too."

Chapter Ten

The silence across the mobile connection was ominous. Kellan's heart pounded as he waited for Rory to reply to his announcement that he was having doubts about the restaurant opening. He gripped the balcony railing with his free hand and stared at the harbor, grasping for any sense of peace from the water.

He'd certainly had peace last night on the boat with Sam. Seeing all kinds of stars, orgasmic and otherwise. Sam knew exactly what to do with his tongue on another man's body.

A seagull landed on the nearest boardwalk lamppost, nearly at eye level with him, staring at him pointedly, as if to say *Peace from the water? Look at you.*

Something that Aoife would say, were she here. The expression on the face of the seagull was kind of like her, too. She'd promised she'd find a way to keep in touch after death. Inhabiting a bird that loved stealing French fries and crapping on cars seemed her style.

He laughed.

"You find this funny?" Rory snapped.

Good Christ, he'd drifted away from the conversation, which deserved his full concentration.

"Ror, I'm so sorry. I got to thinking about Aoife, and there was a seagull, and—"

His friend hummed sympathetically. "At least your memories of her have you smiling."

"Sure." He swallowed. "I didn't call to chat about my grief, though."

"Something tells me it's intrinsically tied to you announcing that you're doubting our business plan. The one we've been busting our arses on for literal years."

Oof. A rough truth, he knew. "It might be."

"Having someone die, love, someone young… It's bound to get you asking questions. But it doesn't mean you need to throw away what mattered before their death. Aoife loved seeing you on the line, or heading out in your whites to accept all that praise. And she'd get a thrill knowing that her money was a big part of getting a bunch of English folks to love something—to *crave* something—unapologetically Irish. Proving we can be upscale, too."

He didn't doubt Rory was right. Sort of. "Aoife would have adored that *if* she knew it was what had my heart on fire. And I just don't know it is."

"Well, figure it out, wouldja? Your bloody self-discovery's been enough of a hit, having you gone for months. And now this…"

"I couldn't get the money without being gone."

"And now you're not sure you want to use it for our plan anyway."

"Rory…"

"We might not share blood," he said, "but we're still family. Not to put too fine a point on it, but the only quality family you have left."

"And that wouldn't change. But I need more than just you, Steven and the kids." One of the reasons they'd decided to stay in London instead of opening a place in Dublin or Cork was Rory's English husband. Rory had wanted their kids to be close to Steven's parents.

"You'll bounce back, darling. Really. We'll build our empire, and you'll get the chance to find someone special now that you won't be at the hospital every night."

"I'm starting to wonder if I could find someone special here. On Oyster Island."

Rory let out a strangled sound. "What now?"

"I'm happy here," he said softly.

"Excuse me, sir, but I'm going to have to ask you to put the real Kellan on the line. Because this isn't him."

Maybe no one knows the real Kellan.

Felt like Sam could see him, though.

Listen to yourself. Throwing away your dreams because of a fine face.

He groaned. "This is bonkers. Sorry. You're right. You're dead right. I'm letting this island bewitch me.

There has to be a way to achieve our goals in London without feeling like I'm running on a hamster wheel."

"Good," Rory said. "Don't scare me like that."

They talked for a few more minutes—Kellan filled his friend in on the progress he'd made diving, and Rory shared his excitement over the weekend, a kid-free holiday he and Steven were planning to Paris in May.

Kellan signed off, promising he'd stop with the illogical thoughts.

Taking care of your health is not illogical.

Aoife again. God, why was she yapping at him so much this morning?

He went for a run, trying to avoid her sound advice. He couldn't switch gears on Rory and their plans.

The trail was on the crowded side for a weekday morning. He ran by packs of hikers and waved at the fellow from the meat counter at the grocer's and a barista who worked at Sam's mum's shop. Even Matias, who was out with Archer. The men had matching black Labradors, and Kellan stopped for some canine scritches and a hello for Sam's friends.

His trainers ate up the miles.

He cooled down by pacing on the boardwalk, fulfillment coming as much from the welcoming people he'd encountered as the endorphins from exercise.

The door opened to the coffee shop and a woman walked out, her gray-blond hair piled on her head and her green eyes—Sam's eyes—sparkling. *Sam's mum.* Rachel, if he remembered correctly. Finally meeting her, then. She held a wrap sweater closed in one hand and carried a tall, plastic cup of water in the other. She made a beeline for him.

Bracing his hands behind his head, he stopped pacing and smiled in greeting, hoping he appeared relaxed. Lies, of course—who wouldn't start sweating as his fella's mother approached?—but he could pretend.

Rachel held out the drink, stopping before she invaded his personal space. "I can see why my son enjoys your company. You've got a smile that could break hearts, Kell Murphy."

She used the nickname Sam did—Sam must have been talking about him.

Warmed by the discovery, he took the offered water and downed half of it. "Thanks a million. I must look a mess if you're out here hand-delivering water."

"Or I needed the excuse to finally meet you *and* come stick my nose in your business."

"Sam didn't give me the impression you ever needed an excuse for that," he teased around another sip.

She laughed and swatted his biceps.

"What business are you looking to stick your nose into?" he asked.

"My son's boat slip was empty outside business hours yesterday."

Using a nearby bench, he started stretching his calves. "And that's unusual?"

"Frankly? Yes."

He nodded. Pumped him up a bit to know that Sam liked him enough to veer from his routine.

"Unusual," Rachel said, "and something I've been hoping for. So keep doing it."

He dropped the stretch, heart sinking. "Rachel... You know I'm not here much longer." Two weekends with a couple more lessons and his test sandwiched between, and then he'd be gone.

"I know." She took the empty glass from him and winked. "But these things have a way of working themselves out. Sometimes, unplanned destinations are the best." Her gaze flicked over his shoulder and her eyes widened. "I'd better get back to the counter. Come have a snack on the house later, if you like. I've been playing with different types of hummus, trying to get through an overabundance of winter greens in my freezer. Maybe you have some secrets you could share."

She rushed off before he could reply.

"Lovely to meet you!" he called to her back. Plus, he never turned down an opportunity to chat about food with other cooks.

Confident steps rapped on the boards behind Kellan, speeding up. "Mom, wait!"

The coffee shop door swung shut.

"Oh, come on," Sam grumbled.

Smiling, Kellan turned and held out a hand. "A mhuirnín."

Sam took his fingers and brought them to his lips, softly kissing them and melting Kellan's heart, all at once. "A warning?"

Laughing, Kellan shook his head. "Uh woor-neen."

He drew out the Gaelic phonetically. "Just a silly endearment. Ignore me."

Or don't, darling.

Not much would hurt more than being ignored by Sam Walker.

"I tried to ignore you," Sam said grouchily. "Tried to work, thinking all day about making you groan my name on the bow of my boat. I managed to control myself until I caught you cooling down from your run in front of my office window, looking like sex on a stick—"

"Sweaty sex," Kellan corrected, his cheeks heating.

"The best kind." Sam's voice lowered to a growl. "Anyway, Franci pushed me out the door because I kept staring out the window and screwing up our monthly invoicing."

Kell grinned. Yes, he definitely liked throwing this man off his game. He slid his fingers into Sam's hair and leaned closer for a peck.

Sam took it deeper than that, cupping the back of Kellan's head and devouring his mouth like he was starving and Kellan was an exquisite-tasting menu.

One of these days, he'd be able to kiss these lips and not have his knees go weak from the sheer perfection of it.

Today was not that day.

Lost track of time, too, until a sharp wolf whistle from the direction of the dock reminded him they were in a very public place.

Kellan pulled back.

Sam let him but reached to hold both his hands.

"Sweet Jesus, I wasn't expecting—" Kellan inhaled, still short on air from the oxygen thief standing before him. "Your mother's probably watching."

"She needs to mind her own business." Sam sighed.

"You're her son. I'd say you are her business," Kellan said. "And she seemed lovely."

"Alyssa didn't think so." Sam cringed, turning pale. "My ex."

"You don't mention her much."

"Figured you wouldn't want to hear about her."

Kellan squeezed Sam's hands. "I want to hear everything that's important to you."

Oof, too much, Murphy.

But Sam seemed unfazed. Happy even, a small smile dancing on the corner of his full mouth. "You're not an average vacation hookup, Kell."

His stomach tensed. *Hookup.*

He'd have to recite those words until his heart got the picture.

And since the whole point of a fling was sex… "What time do you get off?"

"Not soon enough."

"You know where to find me. If you're free, that is." Stealing Sam away for two consecutive nights was probably too much to ask.

"You make me want to be." Regret flashed in sea-green eyes. Sam hesitated for a second, then walked away.

You make me want that, too.

Couldn't blame that voice on his dead sister. The

temptation to cancel his fast-approaching flight and stay on Oyster Island was all his own.

Kellan fought with numbers for the rest of the day and well past sundown, trying to figure out a business structure that would allow him a more balanced lifestyle once he returned home. He at least looked up to notice that unlike last night, there were no brilliant colors to savor—the horizon had been a bank of gray cloud that slowly darkened to black. No stars, either. He and Sam had picked the right night to compare Kell's flimsy understanding of astronomy to Sam's much more impressive knowledge.

And much like Cassiopeia had swum in Kellan's vision when, long after dusk, Sam had knelt and pushed him to the very edges of pleasure, the numbers on his computer spreadsheet were squiggling now. He emailed Rory the revised earning projections he'd been struggling with and shut his laptop.

Tossing his reading glasses on the makeshift desk, he stood and stretched, and went to the other side of the kitchen island to find something to eat.

Fine, to stress eat.

Running a hand over the growling, not-overly flat stomach that Sam seemed to like just fine, thank you very much, he looked in the refrigerator. He really should have gone down to Hideaway Bakery to take Rachel up on her offer of hummus.

He really wished Sam had taken him up on his offer of coming to find him after work.

Couldn't blame the bloke for being tired after a

work shift and then another doing whatever running around his dad and sisters asked of him.

Yanking a bundle of kale from the crisper—he'd plucked the veg from the still-sparse offerings at Saturday's farm market by the ferry terminal—he got to ripping off leaves, then peeled the spines. A bit of vinegar, salt and sugar, and they'd make a nice pickle after chilling in the fridge for a week.

You'll have to eat them quickly. Unless you stick around longer.

Ah, Aoife. He knew she'd be back.

"I'll leave them with Sam," he muttered to the empty kitchen.

A knock on the door.

He startled, banging his knee on the island. "Damn it!" He limped to the door, hating how he wished it was Aoife on the other side, hating how it couldn't be.

Kellan opened the door. "You'll do instead," he blurted, then cursed at the confusion and disappointment on Sam's face.

"What?"

"I—" Best to tell the truth. "I'm after wishing it was my sister knocking. It…" He swallowed, trying to shrink the lump growing in his throat. "I'll be fine for days, and then, I'm just not."

A blur of efficient movement had the door closed, the stovetop shut off, a jacket cast on a chair and Kellan pulled to the couch, ensconced in a strong pair of arms. Loving arms.

"I doubt I'm the first to say that grief isn't linear, but it's true," Sam said.

"It's worth repeating." Nuzzling muscles honed by hours underwater was quickly becoming one of Kellan's favorite pastimes. "You didn't text."

"Thought I'd surprise you."

"And you found me all melancholic-like. Apologies."

Sam glanced at the kitchen. "Melancholy makes you break out the...kale?"

"I pickle when I'm sad."

"There are worse habits." Sam's hand circled, circled, circled, soothing beyond what Kellan thought possible. "I've never had pickled kale."

"If it fits in a jar, I've poured brine on it."

"Last year—almost two years ago, it was before the accident—I was in Vancouver with friends. We went to this restaurant, probably as fancy as the one you're planning to build because I nearly had to take out a loan to pay the bill. Anyway, they had this cold rolled chicken thing, and it had pickled rhubarb around it, and I nearly died at the table, it was so good."

"Roulade? Ballantine?"

"Something like that."

"Rhubarb should be ready to harvest in a month or so, here. I could make something similar for you," Kellan mused.

Sam's arms tightened. "You won't be here in a month."

"True. I'll be in Japan."

"And you don't sound excited. Still scared of the diving?"

No, actually. But if he admitted how little he wanted to leave Oyster Island or how little he wanted to be one step closer to being back in London, it would break their agreement to keep feelings out of this. "Have you seen the size of the sharks there, Samuel?"

"Not in person, but God, I'd love to."

"I've a yen to take you with me."

It was the kind of offhand thing a person would say when they knew the wish was impossible and they were trying to make the recipient feel better.

He meant every word of it.

"You'd really want to share a grass hut with me on a beach somewhere?"

"I saw how hot you looked above me on a boat." The sunset had cast Sam's face in sexy shadows, but Kellan had barely noticed it, he'd been so desperate to feel truly connected. He could exaggerate, though, the impact of the physical. "I don't see how you'd look any less attractive with a thatched roof as your backdrop." He smirked for good measure. "So long as you were about to put your mouth on me."

Sam's smile faltered. "Ah, yeah. Glad you enjoyed that."

He had, but didn't like how Sam was frowning. Maybe hiding from their emotional connection wasn't the way to go. Standing, he tugged Sam's hand to follow.

"It's more than that," he admitted. "Kissing you is grand, but if we were holidaying together, it would be your company I enjoyed the most."

Sam's frown stayed put. "Either way, I can't go."

"I know." Kellan backed up a step, toward the bedroom door. "But it doesn't feel right to pretend I'm only doing this because you turn me on. You've a way of making a man care about you."

Sam stayed rooted in place. "You weren't supposed to do that. Care about me."

"You let me worry about my feelings." He wasn't going to lie and say he'd be fine—he damn well wouldn't—but he wasn't going to hold back, either.

"It's what I do, Kellan. I worry."

"Oh, I know." He stepped back another meter, dislodging Sam from his rigid stance, and kept going, praying he didn't run into something as he walked in reverse. But he didn't want to risk breaking his gaze with Sam, lest it gave the other man an excuse to retreat. "You hover and coddle and indulge people. And I wouldn't expect you to leave your family when they need you, not for a month, or any length of time. But while I'm here—" His knees hit the back of the bed.

Sam kept moving forward, a wall of heat seaming against him. "While you're here...?"

"Let me care about you, will you?" Kellan said.

"What does that look like?"

"Enjoying more than sex with you, Sam."

"I... I have one idea," Sam said, biting and releasing his lip.

"Oh?"

"A few of the harbor restaurants, including Mom and Win's bakery and The Cannery, have a spring meal they put on together. A progressive dinner. It's on Friday. Would you like to come? It's sold out, but

I know a guy, bet I could get you a ticket and bring you as my date."

"Your date." The invitation made Kellan melt a bit.

Sam blinked nervously.

"I'd love to be your date, Sam," Kellan said. "I fancy you, in case you hadn't noticed."

Strong hands gently pushed him to the mattress.

He grabbed the front of Sam's shirt and pulled him in, flipping his built, diver's body and pressing him into the squishy duvet.

"I get that feelings make a man vulnerable," Kellan said. "Even so. Take a risk on me. Please."

Sam's throat bobbed. "Goddamn, I miss this mattress."

Not ready to agree, then. Kellan didn't love that, but it wasn't going to stop him from taking advantage of Sam being here.

He stripped off Sam's hoodie, exposing a fitted gray vest. "Allow me to reacquaint you with its memory-foam charms."

"Hell yeah."

"No fear of losing clothes overboard here." Five quick button flicks from Sam's nimble fingers, and his shirt fluttered to the floor. They were a blur of limbs, of tearing off Sam's jeans. A quick laugh as Kellan took in the cartoon octopi printed on the pants beneath. They sailed across the room.

The man had a chest made for tasting, and getting to touch and lick and soak in the scent of salty breeze overwhelmed Kellan. How was it possible to want someone this much? To know, just *know*, the best ways to make Sam groan and sigh, but also to feel like there were a thousand unknown sources of pleasure to explore?

"I could do this for days," Kellan said.

Sam ground his hips up. "I could let you."

Ugh, too much anticipation, shimmering along Kellan's skin, addictive but hinting at something even better, spurring him to more.

"You're the one who showed up on my doorstep. Your doorstep." His laugh came out a croak. "You know what I mean. What suits your fancy?"

"I want…" Sam kissed a meandering trail down Kell's throat, nipping oh so good along the tender skin. "I want to be inside you. Does that work for you?"

"Very much. Can I ride you?"

"Yeah."

"Kiss me first."

Sam did more than that, pulling Kellan under a spell, taking off his clothes and touching him everywhere but the tight ring of muscles he'd promised to penetrate.

"I want this to be good for you, too." He gripped Sam's shaft, circling the head with his thumb.

Sam inhaled sharply. "It will be."

"You might decide I'm a lousy ride," Kellan said lightly.

Sam cracked up. "I already know you aren't."

"I appreciate the confidence." He straddled Sam's erection. His eyes crossed and he grunted, guttural. Too revealing, probably.

Sam's laughter shifted to a quiet, amazed chuckle. "Enjoying yourself?"

Kellan rocked again, savoring every ounce of pressure. "Sorry. I'm shameless."

A quick stroke of his own length had him groaning even louder.

"I love it," Sam said.

I could love you.

The thought froze Kellan in place.

"What?" Sam stared up, his wavy hair a mess from Kellan's fingers. "Problem?"

"Ah—course not."

"Good." Sam's smile was easy as he nicked some lube from the bottle on the nightstand. "I love watching you like this, too."

Sneaking his hand between their pressed-together bodies, Sam traced Kellan's entrance with a fingertip.

"A chroí, that's—" The finger pressed past his resisting muscles, lighting him on fire and stealing the rest of his words.

"Never know what you're mumbling with the Gaelic."

You don't want to know, my heart.

He braced his palms on Sam's shoulders and tipped forward. Only more fingers, more tender strokes would be enough.

If there was such a thing as enough.

Sam seemed endless.

And who could blame Kellan for wanting endless—

A storm swept across his prostate. He whimpered, clutching Sam's shoulders and falling forward. His face was in the crook of Sam's neck and the smell of the skin there pulled him further under.

Sam kissed his temple and added another finger.

Kell melted toward oblivion.

"There it is. Took long enough to get you out of your head," Sam said.

"Your bad habits—" Kell swallowed, his voice a bare rasp "—are brushing off on me."

"Can't have that." Sam's whisper kissed his ear. "You feel relaxed."

"I am."

Sam withdrew his hand. "I need my jeans."

Nearly whining at the loss of the brilliant fullness, Kellan searched in the bedside table. "I've got us covered."

He fussed with the foil packet, sheathing Sam. Two slow thrusts of his fist and Sam's eyes fluttered shut. Kellan was desperate to share the sensation. He gripped them both, pumped, captured Sam's low moan with a gentle kiss.

"You make some pretty noises, too, like."

"Yeah, well—" the kiss turned frantic "—you make me forget myself."

"Mmm, same."

Kellan loosened his grip and rose on his knees, and oh lord, if he'd thought Sam's fingers were perfect as they swirled and nudged, he'd not properly accounted for how much better his erection would be.

He sank slowly, sucking in a breath as pressure shifted to burn.

"Too much?" Sam said, voice strained.

"Ha, no."

Kellan's reality was tipping, the dark embrace of release already edging his vision.

Fingers dug into either side of his hips. "Too *little?* Ouch."

"Shut up, Sam." Best way to make that happen was to kiss the man. He nipped at Sam's full lower lip, then soothed it with his tongue. "Too *good.*"

Sam's mouth curved under Kellan's. "I thought so."

"So stop joking. You're exactly what I need."

Hips snapped, sending Kellan's world dancing. "Kellan. Sweetheart. I can't…"

Sweetheart.

Heart skipping, he reached for his own length. Sam got there first, a thick palm stroking him closer to the clouds.

Clarity slipped away, the edges of the world softening. Everything was hands and thrusts, heat and pleasure and build until everything sharpened, fractured. Sam groaned, arching, spinning the kaleidoscope around Kellan even faster.

He fell against Sam's chest, ears roaring. His upper body rose and fell as Sam inhaled and exhaled.

"Sorry. I made a mess of you. I'll move, promise," he said.

"Don't." Sam looped his arms around Kellan's back. "Stay another minute. Haven't gotten enough of you, yet."

Chapter Eleven

Sam blinked awake, his heart racing for the span of time it took him to place where he was. Not that it took long, though. Only one possibility, given the sexy man draped half across him.

"Kell. I fell asleep."

"It's still dark," Kell murmured. "Being asleep is the point."

"I have to get back to my dad's." Irritation crawled along his skin. He missed living in his own place. *This* place.

Kissing Kell's sharp cheekbone, he groaned. "Sorry I can't stay. You—I'm choked we can't share coffee and watch the sunrise."

"Sleep through the sunrise, you mean."

"Next time," Sam promised. "Whatever you want."

"Right, next time." Pulling the covers around his

chin, Kell nuzzled into his pillow and closed his eyes. "Text me when you get home safe."

"Now who's hovering?"

A snore was his only answer.

Another kiss to Kell's cheek, a scramble for his clothes, and Sam was out the door and in his truck, squinting into the darkness. It was a short drive, but it took him through the intersection of the accident. There was no way to avoid the corner. Only one road connected the small village at Hideaway Wharf to the horseshoe-shaped road to the rest of the island. And every time he paused at the three-way stop, he was overcome by a strange combination of needing to slow down out of paranoia a car might T-bone him and wanting to speed up so he didn't have to be there any longer than necessary.

Those plants on top of the play structure...

Chest clenching, he drove the last few blocks and pulled into the driveway of his childhood home. His headlights caught movement heading for the back porch. Cane-wielding movement.

He slid from the truck and slammed the door, a warning in case it wasn't who he thought it was. "Dad?"

Crap, why was his father out in the dark?

Sam jogged around the side of the house. The back porch was empty, but a familiar shadow lurked on the other side of the door, outline visible through the thin curtain covering the wide glass panel.

He opened the door, catching his dad's retreat into the kitchen. After toeing off his sneakers, he followed.

His dad's teeth were set and his jaw ticked. He gripped the kitchen counter and hissed out a breath. Classic Greg Walker, pushing through the pain. His cane leaned against the dishwasher door.

"What's wrong?" Sam asked. "You weren't out looking for me, were you?"

"Muscle cramp." Greg dug a thumb into the back of his thigh. "And no, I wasn't looking for you."

Sam pulled out the coffee pods, a rote habit, and loaded the machine and his dad's mug. "Why are you up so early?"

"Same reason you are."

"But I was with—" Wait. The easiest way to get from their neighbor's to their house was through the back door. His jaw dropped. "You slept with Alice Chang?"

"Just Ali, to me." Dad was grinning, despite his obvious leg pain.

Oh, hell, was that why he had a cramp?

"You're having sex with our neighbor?"

"No, I'm *seeing* our neighbor." Greg chuckled. "The sex is a bonus."

Sam groaned, trying to focus on the first thing that came to mind that wasn't his dad getting it on with the friendly, middle-aged widow next door. "You just left Charlotte in the house alone."

Greg sighed. "Charlotte's seventeen, Sammy. She doesn't need a babysitter. If she ran into trouble, she knew how to find me."

Wait, his sister knew about this? Why hadn't she told him? "I should have been here."

"Why?" His dad accepted the offered coffee. "You were all of five minutes away."

"What if you fell?"

"Then—if it wasn't something Ali or Charlotte could help me with—I'd have to wait five minutes for you to get here."

"It's not that simple, Dad."

"I beg to differ, son. A year ago, months ago even, yeah, it would have been more of a problem. But I'm getting a better handle on my pain. The Reiki and the PT are helping. And Ali and I have been learning tai chi together. Her mother swears by it."

He tried to picture his dad and their no-nonsense neighbor moving in tandem next to Alice's meticulously trimmed hydrangeas. The image didn't materialize right away, but it wasn't impossible to envision.

"Might be time for you to get your life back, Sam," Greg said softly.

"I haven't given up my life."

"You've made sacrifices."

Sam's throat went tight. Kell had claimed that, and now his dad, too… "You would have done it for me."

"In a heartbeat." His dad made a face. "It's been rough. For all of us."

"You could say that. I hated—hate—seeing you in pain. And I couldn't take it away. I needed to do something."

"You've done everything, son. Don't think I don't see that. And I'm not back to where I was. Won't ever be. Starting to get good with that. Yeah, I have my bad days where I can't do much. But I'm having more good days. And I happen to like hanging out in Ali's yard on those days. And she has a way of making the bad days better, too."

"How have you been sleeping together without me noticing? I live here, for God's sake."

"I noticed." There was an edge to his dad's voice, part humor, part annoyance. "But tonight was the first night I decided to stay over."

"The first night *I* ended up staying somewhere else."

"Well, yeah. Didn't feel like having to ask my son's permission to romance a woman and I knew you'd get cranky if I wasn't in my own bed."

Swearing, Sam rubbed his face with both hands. "Sorry to cramp your style."

Greg squeezed his shoulder. "Feeling's mutual. Worried the accident wrecked your marriage, to be honest."

"Alyssa and I wrecked our marriage just fine by ourselves," he said wryly. "She was never happy with island life."

His dad took a long sip of coffee. "Are you?"

"Of course. I love running the shop and being close to our family."

"Might want to find someone to share that with, though."

"Yeah, maybe." After Kell left, after he moped and sulked and got over losing such an incredible man, maybe he'd start dating more seriously. Try to find someone local. Someone he could trust not to leave.

Except I know everyone local. And none of the eligible people are half as fine as Kell Murphy.

* * *

There was a difference between standing on the boat platform only in a dry suit, preparing for a swim, and standing there with a tank strapped to his back. Days after his first swimming practice, Kellan was back on Sam's boat, ready to test out the beginning of a controlled descent. Sam wanted him to get used to the feeling of deflating his buoyancy control device and slowly descending below the surface. Kellan was just happy with taking things slow. He'd had another online therapy session, reviewing his arsenal of anti-anxiety techniques. Trusted Sam implicitly as his instructor, too. The second Kellan had a problem, Sam would support him surfacing.

The neoprene of the wet suit clung to Kellan's body, the tight neck of the hood constricting his breathing.

No, that's my fear doing that. I can breathe just fine.

He shifted under the burden of his equipment. The steel tank, the heavy weight belt. The BCD, which he'd inflate and deflate to balance out the pull of gravity, seemed small and pathetic.

Once he stepped into the water, what if he kept sinking?

Or I'll float. And then I'll swim. I'm in control.

"We're twenty feet deep here, Kellan," Sam said, floating a few feet from the platform. His easy treading suggested not a care in the world, but the lines at the corners of his mouth were all concern.

Concern for Kellan, no doubt, because he had to look a fright. Going off the tingle in his cheeks, his complexion was no doubt the white of the puffy anemones below.

The water was green, the sand and rock of the bottom visible. Shallow.

His fear aside, he knew it wouldn't feel any different from descending in the pool. He'd practiced in the pool with a thick, cold-water wet suit so that there wouldn't be any surprises.

"Weight check?" Sam said.

He'd done the math for his weight belt a dozen times, accounting for body weight and the thickness of his suit, his boots and hood, the tank, the salt water… "Twenty-one pounds." He ran through his reasoning for Sam.

Sam grinned. "I know. Just making sure you do. And reminding you that you know what you're doing."

"If you say so."

"If you can cook for famous people, you can handle a little depth and pressure."

Having the confidence of others did always make it easier. He sucked in a breath and fidgeted with the straps on his BCD. "One night, half the *Bridgerton* cast came in. After I got over how bloody pretty they all are, I started sweating. Felt a lot like this, really."

"I bet they loved their dinner."

"Sure, they all sent back their compliments and asked to see me." The picture he'd had taken with them was still on the office wall.

"What got you through that?"

Ah, that's where Sam was going with this. "My

training. Knowing I'd made truffle consommé with puff pastry a thousand times before."

"Would you make that for me sometime?" Sam looked ready to drool.

"This isn't the same," Kellan said, exasperated. "I've only done this in the pool a few times. Shocking really, how little a person learns before they strap on a tank and jump in. How do more people not die?"

"Because they have instructors watching them," Sam said, his calm correction the opposite of Kellan's panicked squeak. "I'm here. If you do want to come in the water with me, I won't let anything happen to you. If you decide today's not the day, that works, too."

Just think, he'd crowed to his therapist how easy last week's swim was, honestly hoping for some praise. As always, she'd kept it about his own reactions. *And how did* you *feel?*

Victorious.

And Sam wasn't wrong to draw a comparison— Kellan *did* feel victorious at the end of a notable service.

Out here on the water, Sam was the head chef. Kellan was back to being a commis chopping veg, the early stuff a chef did as they worked their way up.

Which was okay. It was okay to be a beginner.

His training told him he'd correctly calculated his equipment and when he stepped in, he'd float until he released the air in his BCD.

His anxiety couldn't out-argue the truth—Sam would make sure he was safe. Equipment failure? Sam knew what to do. Snag under water? He could get Kellan free. Even a first aid emergency—he was trained for that.

And he was as passionate and committed to getting Kellan in and out of the water incident-free as Kellan was when he'd placed shaved discs of black truffle onto soup for a group of world-famous actors.

With trust humming in his veins, Kellan ran through the giant stride checklist. When he was certain he'd remembered all the points, he stepped off the platform.

Sank down a little, but didn't keep going. A second later, his head broke the surface. He started to sink again, so he inflated his BCD to the necessary level.

Calm and steady on the surface. This was good.

Sam was a couple of meters away. "Slow breaths. Preserve your tank."

Kellan nodded.

They'd talked over and over about the technicalities. He knew what to do.

He popped the regulator out. "Let's go farther than five feet. I want to check out the bottom."

Sam's mask didn't hide his surprised blink. "We can do that if you're ready. Not much to see here, though."

Kellan peered around the side of the boat out toward the nearest point in the cove. "What if we descended and then swam out?"

"If you're feeling prepared for that."

"I am."

"Okay. You know what to do if you need to surface at any time. We'll descend together almost to the bottom, establish neutral buoyancy, and then swim out as far as you're comfortable with. We'll stop every five feet of depth, until we reach forty feet."

"Could this count as one of my four dives?"

"If we make that depth, yeah."

He floated up on a wave and down again. "Let's aim for that."

"You got it. Just communicate, and don't feel bad about cutting it short. The only thing we'll practice this time, other than the descent, is safety stops on the way up. We don't need them for this depth, but you might as well show me you can do them. Nothing fancy."

There were a bunch of skills he'd have to perform to officially pass his certification, and he appreciated not having to worry about them right now. Sharing a regulator might be a bridge too far for today.

"Ready?"

"Steady, go," Kellan finished, following Sam's lead in letting air out of his BCD.

They sank slowly.

He couldn't see any part of Sam's face besides his eyes behind his mask. Pressure built in his ears. He equalized and then checked his depth gauge. Ten feet.

Sam made the okay sign. Bubbles rose around his face as he exhaled.

Kellan returned it, letting the hiss and whoosh of his own breath soothe like a meditation. It was okay. The mirror-like reflection of the surface above. The hull of the boat and the propeller. And the bottom, clearer now, a sandy swath broken up by a few rocks here and there.

At fifteen feet, Kellan followed Sam's lead in inflating his BCD so that he could hover, weightless. He knew he could stay there if he wanted. A thrill ran through him as he stared out to the distance, green fading to black as far as he could see. Partly the anxious bite of the unknown. But the excitement of possibility, too.

He flashed Sam the okay sign and pointed toward the depths.

The underwater terrain didn't change much from twenty feet to twenty-five, twenty-five to thirty. The light did, though. They passed a clump of rock that had an occupant, a Dungeness crab going about her day. What was brilliant red on the reef near the surface was a muted brick color.

Still the prettiest thing he'd seen on his travels.

The view of the Andes from the peak of Aconcagua had nothing on accomplishing something he'd not thought he could do a mere three weeks ago.

His breaths came faster, and he forced himself to slow down. He wasn't going to run out of air—they wouldn't be down here long enough to get close to emptying the tank—but he knew he needed to establish good habits.

Kellan checked his depth gauge, noted thirty-five feet, and stopped swimming like they'd agreed.

Sam paused, too. Held up five fingers. Took his regulator out and mouthed two words.

Five more, maybe.

Anticipation ripped through him. So close.

He motioned for Sam to follow and carefully watched their descent. *Thirty-seven. Thirty-nine.*

Two more kicks, and then *forty-one.*

Sam held up a fist, clearly waiting for a fist bump. As Kellan knocked their knuckles together—no such thing as momentum underwater—Sam tangled their gloved fingers together and held tight.

Screw a delicious crustacean. *Sam Walker* was the prettiest thing Kellan had ever seen.

And he needed to do something to make sure next week's farewell wasn't forever.

Sam's fingers tightened, and he motioned for Kellan to look behind him.

A pair of round black eyes and a whiskered nose poked through golden brown ribbons of kelp swaying in the water.

Kellan froze. A seal. *Shite.* Those things had to weigh one or two hundred kilos.

Putting a hand on Kellan's upper arm, Sam kicked a bit, repositioning to his side.

Holding out his fist, he stuck out a thumb and rotated it from side to side, then made a thumbs-up and a thumbs-down motion, then a palm out.

Which way? Go up, go down, stop.

Kellan could barely keep his eyes on the signals—he had to watch the animal. He'd seen videos where seals would play with divers, pull on the tubes of their air source or tug on mask straps or hoods. His breath was like a fireplace bellows in his ears.

Sam waved a flat hand up and down.

Calm down.

The seal swam forward a few feet, its spotted body hovering in the water, free of the kelp.

Too many bubbles floated around Kellan's face.

He'd gone over this with his therapist yesterday. Rule number one: controlled breaths. She'd had him visualize it. Stuck? Keep breathing. Scared? Keep breathing. Heart rate rising? Keep breathing. Be Dory from *Finding Nemo*, essentially.

But they'd not covered seals.

Sam touched his arm again, then made the okay sign.

A question, probably, because no doubt Sam was fine. He'd probably swam with seals hundreds of times, and—

Hundreds of times. And he's fine.

If I stick with him, I'll be fine, too.

That was enough to get Kellan's shoulders down from up by his ears, to relax his intercostal muscles and take in a slow, full breath. Then another.

The seal came closer.

Kellan pointed at it, then made the okay sign.

Reaching one hand toward the seal and weaving his fingers through Kellan's with the other, Sam held otherwise still.

Might as well follow suit.

They floated in the water, waiting for the animal's decision.

It glided forward, approaching Sam's outstretched hand.

Nosing the neoprene-covered fingers.

What the *what*?

This couldn't be real. It was objectively terrifying and unreal...

And spectacular.

The animal fit no other word. Smooth lines and curious eyes and yikes, look at those claws, poking out of the ends of its front flippers.

The animal curved one of those flippers around Sam's fingers.

Sam copied the gesture, bending his gloved hand around the surprisingly soft-looking paddle, then reached up to scratch the side of the animal's head, like a dog.

Kellan tasted salt. Oh, damn. In his shock, he'd let his jaw hang. His regulator dangled from his lips.

Muscle memory kicked in, and he breathed like he was spitting to clear the valve, releasing extra bubbles.

The seal pulled its flipper away from Sam's hand and swam up and around like a rollercoaster loop-de-loop, settling a few feet away again.

No, don't go.

Kellan held out his free hand toward the creature.

His other fingers were still wrapped tight in Sam's, anchoring him better than the thick chain that fixed the boat to the bottom.

Come on, come say hello. Say hello so I can tell Aoife all about it.

Even if telling his sister just involved talking to himself.

Heart tugged between grief and the knowledge this

was a once-in-a-lifetime experience, Kellan squeezed Sam's hand and waited for the seal to respond.

Back flippers paddling tentatively, it crept forward again, bumping the side of its head into Kellan's offered palm.

He could have shouted with joy, but that would create more bubbles to scare the animal away, and also risk losing his air source. *No thank you.* He waited.

The seal glided along his arm, then darted away, skimming its belly along the sand-and-crushed-shell bottom before disappearing back behind the kelp and into the forever green.

Sam rotated, palming one side of Kellan's hood-covered head. Taking out his regulator, he leaned in and kissed the small triangle of exposed skin on Kellan's cheek. Then he tapped his wrist and made a thumbs-up sign.

Go up?

But how, when it was a miracle down here, and...

You're welcome, Kellan love.

His subconscious, mimicking what he wished his sister could say. But down here, the otherworldly green, the no-less-than-magical encounter—he could believe he was capable of getting messages from the beyond. Whether the words were about the seal or Sam's brief kiss, he didn't know.

He was thankful for both.

He didn't want to leave, not Sam, not this incredible experience.

And once he figured out the best way to put that into words, he was going to tell Sam how he felt.

Chapter Twelve

Sam threw open the shop's back door. It hit the wall. One of the framed pictures from his outdated "dream destinations" wall fell to the floor, a map of Indonesia marked with five dive sites he'd planned to visit with his dad one day. The glass cracked.

He dropped the large dive bag and set down his tank apparatus, then placed the picture on top of a filing cabinet, shooting a rueful smile at Kell, who followed a few feet behind. It was unlikely he was going to get to Indonesia any time soon.

"Oh dear," Kell said.

Sam lifted a shoulder. "Hard to contain myself. The seal, you finishing a *second* dive and being an absolute all-star underwater—" plus the quickie on the captain's chair once they were out of their wet suits "—it doesn't get better than that." He slid his hand along Kell's cheek and stole a peck. He had to get in as many as he could before Kell drove his rental car onto the ferry next week.

"I wouldn't use the term 'all-star' yet," Kell said. "I didn't do well when you tested me on retrieving my regulator and taking off my tank underwater."

"You completed the skill, nerves or not."

"It was a bloody load of nerves." Kell scanned the collection of maps—places Sam hadn't been yet—and pictures he'd taken underwater in the eight trips he and his dad had taken since they put the wall together a decade ago.

"Those nerves are normal," Sam said. "We'll keep practicing until you feel in control. If that's what you want."

"I do. Want that. And more than that, I want—"

"Sam?" Archer's voice boomed from the sales floor. "You back?"

"I am!" Groaning, eager to hear Kell's list of wants but knowing this wasn't the right place, or at least not the right time, he grabbed his discarded gear and followed his employee's voice. "You won't freaking believe it, Arch! You want luck of the Irish? Talk to this guy. Dive one, we saw—"

Archer's scowl stopped Sam in his tracks, only matched by a miserable look on his sister's face. The duo was side by side behind the counter. Archer's dog was the only one in the room who looked happy to see Sam, his thick black tail thumping the floor. Honu wore a big grin on his furry face as he leaned against Franci's leg. Her fingers kneaded the dog's head and ears.

Sam had been planning on heading straight through to hose off their gear in the equipment room, but one look at Franci's pale complexion and he stopped.

Archer, arms crossed over his wide chest, muttered something in Franci's ear. His tattoos rippled under the turned-up cuffs of his short-sleeved T-shirt. A muscle ticked in his jaw. His Coast Guard training made him impossible to read when he wanted to keep his thoughts to himself. "Whatever you saw can't come close to—"

"Shut up, Archer." Franci hunched forward, hands braced on the edge of the counter, looking like death on a stick. A person could call her wan if they were in an overly Victorian mood.

Honu whined and licked her hand.

All Sam's alarm bells started jangling. "What's wrong?"

A strong hand stroked Sam's back.

Kell had followed, so quietly that Sam hadn't noticed. *Or you get tunnel vision.*

That, too. But who wouldn't, when their sister was as white as the T-shirts on display?

"Fran, what's going on? I thought you said your back was getting better."

"Let me worry about me." Her smile was made of Tupperware plastic. "And I was on time for my shift. Not that you were here to see it."

Anger boiled, sudden and scalding. "I was on a scheduled dive with a paying customer."

Franci snorted in clear disbelief.

She wanted to do this? Fine.

Sam glanced at Kellan and mouthed a preemptive *sorry*. "Look, I won't pretend Kell and I aren't seeing each other. But that doesn't interfere with me taking him on the trips he hired me for." He couldn't stop the flow of words. "I wouldn't do this with just anyone, but... But Kell..." *He's more. More than I expected.* The way he'd worked through his stress today was so fucking impressive. "It's not like we're lawyers or medical professionals. We don't operate under those kinds of ethical boundaries. Hell, you hooked up with that corporate HR dude from Boise a couple of months back."

Franci paled another shade lighter. "Yeah, don't remind me."

Archer let out a sound close to a growl. If gazes were poison darts, Sam would be passed out on the floor right about now.

Sam shot Kell another apologetic smile. He'd thought they'd roll in, clean up, maybe go have a bite to eat to celebrate two successful dives and a half-completed criteria list.

Holding a fist to her mouth, Franci grabbed her purse from under the counter. Goddamn, she looked ill. "Well, this is fun and all, but I need to go help your mom and Winnie get set up for the progressive dinner tonight."

"Are you well enough to be on the waitstaff?" Sam asked, feeling guilty he was going to the dinner with Kell as his date instead of pitching in for his mom.

"If you need help, Francine, you know you can lean on me, right?"

Her face twisted in exasperation on her way out the door. "I know what I can and can't do, Sam. I don't care if you're sleeping with half our client list. I do care about how you make me feel like I can't manage my own life. Trust me for once. Please."

The door swung shut, and it took everything Sam had to lock it for the night instead of following her and probing further. *See, Franci? Here's me, letting you manage your own life.* Hanging his head, he sighed, smacking the wall with a flat palm.

"Uh, Sam?"

He turned, forcing a smile.

"Do you want the bags in the equipment room?" Kell asked gently.

"I've got it. That's what you hired me for."

Stubbled jaw gaping, Kell humphed and hauled his *and* Sam's gear into the equipment room.

"Kell, I didn't mean…" He swore. Repeated it, louder.

Archer loomed next to the POS, stone faced and stiff shouldered.

"Go easy on your sister," he said. Ordered, really.

Sam fisted his hands. "Go easy on her *for what*?"

Archer shook his head and rubbed his thigh above his prosthetic. "Might also want to stop making it sound like you're only spending time with your boyfriend because he paid you to."

"Boyfriend?" Sam grumbled. Couldn't bring himself to say *he's not*, though.

"Tell you what. I'll take off, and you can grovel in private."

"Take off, screw off—either works."

"Love you, too, buddy."

Sam stomped into the equipment room. A few seconds later, he heard the front door shut and the lock click.

Kell knelt on the linoleum flooring, stacking suits, boots and hoods next to the rinsing station.

Sam joined him, plunking down cross-legged between Kell and the pile. "Sorry. That was awkward, and a lot of it was on me." He rested his elbows on his knees and scrubbed his face with both hands, groaning.

A supportive hand squeezed his shoulder, then started rubbing his back. "Something tells me she was poking at you being out with me to distract you from whatever conversation we walked in on between her and Archer."

"And I fell for it."

Kell lifted a corner of his mouth. "Is it still bothering you, sleeping with a person who's your customer?"

"No." Then why had he made so many excuses? "I dunno, not really. Though I don't want people to get the wrong impression about me as a business owner."

"I think everyone on Oyster Island knows you're an upstanding bloke, Sam." The assurance came with a soft smile that made Sam ache all over. Not sexually, for once. The kind of ache that made you want to crawl inside a person, nestle in their chest and let their heartbeat soothe away all the stings and scratches of the day.

"I'm hoping *you* think I'm that, too," Sam said.

"Of course." Staring at the floor, Kell shifted from his knees to his butt, crossing his legs like Sam's. He dropped his hand from Sam's back and laced his fingers in his lap.

A wave of exhaustion swept in with the broken contact. Sam groaned.

"What's wrong?" Kell asked.

He needed to practice that tone, all softness and kind compassion. Get away from the barks and snaps he too often used. "I don't know if it's a post-adrenaline lull or what, but I'm just...tired."

Kell nodded and patted his lap.

Assuming Archer had left as promised, Sam lay down with his head in Kell's lap. He stared at upside-down gray eyes and let someone else carry some of the weight.

Gentle fingers toyed with his salt-stiff hair, tracing teasing patterns on his scalp. "I like taking care of you."

"Feels good on this end, too." He exhaled. "All I meant to do was keep them safe. Safe and happy. They aren't, though. Not from anything I've done, anyway."

"I doubt that's true."

"I owe it to them to stop hovering," Sam said.

"That would leave a man with time on his hands."

"It might..." Was it time to start crossing dreams off his own list?

But Oyster Island and diving were a key part of his life.

Kell had seen a small part of that today, in a damn magical way.

"Up until I completely mishandled that argument with my sister, today was a banner day." The smile on Kell's face when they'd surfaced could have powered the whole island for a month. "That seal made you a diver for life, didn't it?"

"Might have." Kell scratched small circles above Sam's ears with his short nails. "Something tells me seals don't come out to play every dive, though."

"No, some trips are more special than others." *Some people are, too. Like you.*

"I want more," Kell blurted, cheeks pinking. "I didn't mean more diving when I said that earlier. I meant more of you. More time, more commitment… More."

Sam's heart caught in his throat, and he garbled out something unintelligible.

"I know, I know—it's too much, too soon." Kell looked almost as pale as Franci had. "But I can't take it back, and I care about you too much to pretend I didn't mean it."

Sam sat up. "I don't know how to make it work."

"I don't either." A dry laugh. "Still want to give it a lash, though."

"But—if we try and I disappoint you…"

"Let me manage my expectations, Sam. We only have so much time on this earth, and it's much better spent diving with seals and shagging over the captain's chair on your boat than wondering what could have been. Than regretting not trying."

His *t*'s were crisp like fallen leaves, rustling across Sam's skin. "I can commit to...well, to not seeing anyone else after you leave. To video calls. Maybe coming to see your new restaurant in London? A short trip? You won't have much time off during the start-up phase."

Or after it. He'd watched Matias open the pub. A fledgling restaurant was no small thing, even if Kell was trying to fix his business plan to better balance work and life.

A shadow crossed Kell's face.

"Will that be enough?" Sam continued, doubts racing. "Of course it isn't."

"Sure, it's a start. Or a continuation, really. I think our start happened the moment I walked into this shop and started begging the universe you'd be the one to teach me."

"And when I shifted my schedule around to free myself up," Sam said. Heat crawled in his belly. How was he so needy already, when they'd had sex little more than an hour ago?

He was getting attached, that's what.

So long as they were seeing each other long distance, he'd only get more hooked.

And then where would he be? In love with someone who lived on a different continent?

"We've got a couple of hours before the appetizer course at the bakery. Let's finish cleaning up and then go to the apartment," he said gruffly.

They rinsed and hung the equipment.

Kell followed him out the boardwalk door and waited while he locked up. "You're frowning, a mhuirnín. Why?"

Sam jammed his keys in his jacket pocket and stacked his hands on his head. "The last time I let myself fall for someone, she left. It's hard not to expect that to happen again, especially when you live eight time zones away."

"Seven, during the summer."

"Ha. Such a difference," Sam said, striding toward the outside staircase that led up to his rental.

Kell caught his arm, slowed him down. "Look. I'm thinking of alternatives for my restaurant. Different ways I could arrange it, make it so I'm not as married to it."

Christ. Marriage. "I did that once. Said vows. Ended up unsaying them."

"I know you did. Fifty percent of us do. But I'm not talking about vows yet. I'm just trying to figure out a way to see your face sometimes."

"Why would you change your plans for me?"

"I'm changing my plans for *me*." Kellan went over to the rail and braced his hands on the wood. "Before I got here, I couldn't see I was unhappy. And being here helped me see it. Somewhere, my sister's laughing at me. One giant I-told-you-so."

"Sisters like saying that."

"Mine never did. Not when she was alive. She was too busy living to be petty about shite like this. I'll give her this one—she earned it." Kell wiped a tear from the inside corner of his eye.

Sam snuck in close, kissing Kell's cheeks, jaw, mouth.

A low, pleasured sound hummed against his lips, shimmering straight down to his belly. He dug his fingers into Kell's hips.

He wasn't the only one getting hard from a breath of a kiss.

Good.

"Let's go upstairs." They weren't going to solve their distance issue tonight, but they could at least find bliss.

Stumbling up the flight, lips fastened and hands groping on each rise, Sam was a damn rock by the time they hit the landing.

Kell fumbled in his pocket. The keys jangled as he took them out with shaking hands.

"Kellan! Honey, wait a second." Sam's mom's voice came from the bottom of the stairs.

Sam couldn't decide if he wanted to swear or laugh.

Kell paused with his key almost in the lock. "Is that you, Rachel?"

Sam peeled his lips off the back of Kellan's neck, barely holding in an irritated grunt.

His mom stood at the bottom of the flight of stairs, hands wringing. "I'm interrupting. I'm so sorry. But Franci—she's got a bug, and I can't have her serving, and my prep cook was going to step in, but she managed to burn her hand right as she was finishing up the streusel and Winnie's over at the pub working with Matias on the mains and I'm alone and in the weeds with the appetizer course—"

"Mom," Sam said, trying out the soothing tone Kell had used on him earlier. "It'll be okay. We'll help." He leaned toward Kellan's ear. "Shoot, sorry—that *is* okay, right?"

"Of course. I watched you in your natural habitat today—now you can see me in mine. Can't promise it'll be as thrilling as a seal encounter—"

"Natural habitat?" Sam cocked an eyebrow. "I *knew* you'd secretly labeled me a selkie."

Kell winked. "Sometimes I wonder, I do."

Rachel was throwing her stress all over the kitchen—discombobulated plates and prep stations, a blender that had sprayed up the side of a cupboard, a tray of blackened, unusable crumbs on a counter. Her young dishwasher was doing a valiant job of keeping on top of dishes as well as trying to chop parsley, but it was clear he was in over his head.

Kellan held his knife roll in one hand and did a quick mental triage of the state of the kitchen. He wasn't planning on picking up on the erratic energy. He could take over the food prep from the dishwasher, who could then deal with cleaning up some of the mistakes that happened when a chef was overwhelmed and rushing. He could manage an appetizer service for fifty—standing instead of seated, no less—in his sleep.

Besides, he was operating under a charmed star

today. Had to be, given those dives. He'd only panicked once on the second one, some long seconds
of fighting his breath when he'd had to release and
retrieve his regulator at depth. He'd recovered fast
enough, though. Enough to think he might actually
complete his certification.

"Okay," he said to Rachel. "Sam's out front setting up—that'll be fixed in a jiff. Tell me more about
these three dishes."

She wrung her hands. "I'm so sorry I interrupted
the two of you. I could tell you were…busy."

Heat crept from his chest to his ears. Life here
was so out in the open sometimes. So often when he
tried for a private moment with Sam, someone else
got in the way.

And it should have pissed him off, annoyed him
at minimum, but it didn't.

The rhythm of life reminded him of his summers
in Youghal with his gran—people caring and pitching in, having messy opinions and interruptions, but
a whole lot of shared joy that filled the soul. It was
just…ease. When people in this community fell,
someone was there to help them back up.

Rachel needed that right now, from him. It made
him feel a part of things in the very best way, as well
as a deep desire to impress the hell out of her. Because she was lovely. Because she was Sam's mum,
and even though "mother-in-law" wasn't nearly in the
cards, he still yearned for her approval.

"You needed us more than we needed to sneak
off," he said. "Tell me how I can best support you.

I'm assuming you'd be better served with a follower, not a leader."

She wiped her hands on her apron and scanned her workspace with a nervous but knowledgeable eye. "The soup's basically done—when it's time, we'll just need to get it into the spoons with the crème fraîche and herb crumb topping. So, the herbs need prepping. A simple salsa verde for the lamb. And I'm super behind on the fresh ricotta blintzes."

Definitely following, then. No bother. Except… "Can I make a suggestion, Chef?"

She tsked. "Start with tossing that formality out the window."

"This is your space, Rachel. I am but your humble minion. Thing is, I've a vat of fiddlehead tapenade I made when I was bored—it would be heavenly with fresh ricotta. May I alter your recipe, or do you want to keep it simpler?"

"You're doing me a favor tonight. If you want to spice things up a little, have at 'er."

Nodding, he jogged to the flat to retrieve the tapenade and some other goodies—his pickled kale stems would be perfect as a soup garnish, if she wanted. Once back in the kitchen, he fell into a rhythm, carefully crafting a hundred of the thin crepe-like rounds. After they cooled, he got to stuffing them. Smear of tapenade. A few slivers of blanched, local white asparagus spears from the greenhouse of a nearby hobby farmer. Quenelle of cheese. Fold, roll, repeat.

"God, you're fast," Rachel said, sailing by with a

tray of golden-brown crumbs. "We're already caught up, and then some."

"Part of that's your son out there. Who knew he'd be so good at transforming the place from intimate cafe to seaside lounge?"

"My Sammy has hidden talents."

He sure does. Kellan held in his chuckle and the knee-jerk impulse to think of all of Sam's talents that Rachel was surely *not* referring to.

"As do you," she said. "Blintz folding, tapenade making, turning my son's head—all good things."

"I'm hoping they are," he replied. "Truly."

"Depends on how often you visit," she said with a wink.

His fingers slipped and he tore one of the blintzes. *Damn.* He tossed the ruined round aside. Even if he did make arrangements to have a better work-life balance, Sam was right. Traveling from London to Washington state was not a short trip.

His throat constricted and he forced himself to breathe. *We'll figure it out.* Besides, this wasn't the time to get in his head. He'd end up wrecking half his blintzes if he didn't watch it.

They worked on the third offering together, with Kellan searing lamb roulades before getting them in the oven to finish cooking. Rachel was finishing up the salsa verde, and the scent of fresh, green herbs filled the kitchen.

He was julienning meticulous strips of pickled kale, the tang of vinegar mixing with the smells of fresh herbs and browning meat in the air, when

Sam strolled into the kitchen. He was a bit sweaty from hauling tables and chairs to the storage room and bringing in bistro tables in their place, cheeks a healthy pink. He slid behind Kellan, chest to back, and mouthed an open, hungry kiss below Kellan's ear.

Lifting on his toes from the shock to the sensitive place, Kellan squeaked and dropped his knife with a clatter. "Oy! You'll have me cutting myself if you don't watch it."

"Have I ever told you how sexy your hands are when you're wielding a knife?"

"No more than yours are when you're reaching to high-five a marine mammal."

Sam hummed a laugh.

The vibration carried clear down to Kellan's toes. He barely held in a gasp.

"I know," Sam lamented. "I'm still wound up, too."

Had not held the gasp in, then. *Oops.*

"This'll be done at eight," Kellan said. "You should go over to Matias's for dinner—no use wasting the ticket. I'll catch up with you after I help your mum clean and get set back up for the morning. Maybe we can catch dessert together, before we go back to the flat."

"Matias can make doggie bags for us. I'll stay, too. Those tables will move back into place faster with more hands." Another kiss to the sensitive place below Kellan's ear. "And later, we can enjoy dessert in private."

"You're rather good at this boyfriend thing, Sam Walker."

"Boyfriend..."

Kellan winced. "If that works for you."

His nerves jangled as Sam paused, ten seconds that dragged for ten hours.

"If we're at the point of being exclusive and planning trips to visit, *boyfriend* makes sense."

Exhaling, Kellan relaxed against Sam's chest. The acceptance tugged at some of his inner knots, loosening the threads of uncertainty. "I didn't think you'd agree."

"I didn't either," Sam murmured. "But I have a hard time resisting you, Kellan Murphy."

"Good." He tilted his face and skimmed his lips across Sam's jaw. "Now, get out of my space so that I can finish this kale."

Sam backed off, grinning as he stole a spear from the uncut pile. He chewed thoughtfully. "Delicious. Who knew?"

Kellan raised an eyebrow. "Well, me."

"*Oui*, Chef," Sam said with a grin, then left the kitchen, still smiling.

An hour later, they were in the thick of service. The fundraiser attendees were in a jovial mood, enjoying their included glass of pink bubbles and wolfing down the three offered dishes. Rachel mingled with the guests, talking up the trays of mini mugs of soup and the bite-size blintzes.

Kellan stood at what would normally be the cash register, cutting the lamb to order.

Praise flooded in.

Best lamb I ever tasted.

I could eat that tapenade with a spoon.

*That soup is like a warm hug, and that pickle...
I'll be dreaming of that pickle.*

He was careful to give all credit to Rachel where
it was due but couldn't help but be chuffed at how
much the guests enjoyed his small contributions. Seeing people enjoy his food in Rachel's cafe was no less
meaningful than getting called out to a table at a fine-
dining restaurant.

A tenth of the stress, too.

He mulled that over while serving up the final fifteen servings of lamb. He'd always thought he'd be a
failure if he changed course. The future he'd meticulously planned for—this trip had blown it to shreds.

Well, losing Aoife had activated the bomb. *We
change course, Kellan. Sometimes find a better destination.*

"Sweetheart," Sam called, "put the knife down.
Come meet my dad."

More people to make a good impression on. Over
the past couple weeks, he'd met some of Sam's friends
but had kept missing his father. Kellan nodded at the
invitation and held up a finger, wanting to clean up his
station first. He dealt with his cutting board and knife
roll, removed his apron and joined the fray at Sam's
side. Sam grabbed his left hand, lacing their fingers
together the second he walked up to the small group.

"Kell, this is my dad, Greg," Sam said.

Sam's father was a thick-framed guy around Kellan's height, the kind of build that would be at home
on Kellan's neighborhood rugby pitch. He had gray-

ing auburn hair and Sam's winning smile. His stance was a little off-balance; he was leaning heavily on the cane he held in his left hand. His rich brown gaze darted to Sam and Kellan's linked fingers before he offered his own hand to shake. "Nice to meet you."

Kellan accepted the friendly greeting. As soon as he released, Rachel sailed by, shoving a glass of pink bubbles into his hand. He lifted his glass, toasting his boss for the evening, and then smiled at Sam's dad. The man seemed unfazed to be at a party hosted by his ex-wife. Did Sam know how lucky he was, having his parents be so congenial with each other?

Of course, he does, given he claims to be the opposite of congenial with his own ex-wife. "Grand to meet you, too. I've seen you in town once or twice but didn't realize who you were."

"I'm the one who has all the dirt on this guy." Greg nudged Sam with an elbow. "And you're the one who makes magic out of kale stalks, apparently."

"All the dirt? You're a useful one to know."

"I can't feed you, but I *can* keep you entertained," Sam's dad said. "I have no end of stories of this guy as a goofy kid. 'Bout all I can do right now. Tell stories." His words came out wistful, but not sad.

"Goofy, like?" Kellan lifted a questioning eyebrow at Sam, who shrugged.

"Sam says you're from London?"

"In residence, anyway, if not spirit."

"Sheesh, Sammy." Greg shook his head knowingly. "You picked a tricky one this time."

"*Dad*," Sam warned softly. His fingers tightened around Kellan's. In apology, or reassurance?

Kellan didn't need either. He'd seen something in Sam's face earlier, a truth and willingness that he had to believe.

"I haven't been to London in forever." Sam's father's tone was all genuine joviality, though his face was a little strained. "Where's the best place to get a pint? And what's good in the West End? If you're a theater fan. Are you? Or museums? Football? Oh, man, I made some good memories in that city. Rachel and I went once before this guy came along." He slapped his son on the shoulder.

Kellan tried to think of the last time he got tickets for a musical or an exhibit or a match or anything. It had been an embarrassingly long time. All he did was work and hit up other places to see what was current.

Which—also work.

"Honestly?" he said. "My favorite place to eat is the chipper down a back lane from my flat. I do love West End shows and catching a Liverpool match when they're playing a London team. Restaurant hours make it tough, though."

He should have been thinking about going home and doing some of those things. Making plans to go on a pilgrimage to Anfield stadium with Rory or seeing a concert or something. If Sam did come to visit, Kellan could show him the time of his life. An excuse to do the super touristy activities that locals disparaged but were secretly curious about. Or they could hop a quick flight and visit his gran's village.

But I'd rather come back here.

Oyster Island was enough for him.

Not just enough. Better.

"If the rest of your food is as good as what you added here tonight, I bet the place to eat is *your* restaurant," Greg said.

"Kell's between restaurants. He's opening a new place soon," Sam said. "Irish fine dining."

He gave Sam's hand a pulse. They needed to talk about that. Kellan was committed financially to that plan, but he no longer saw himself juggling six saucepans on the top-of-the-line gas range he and Rory had priced out. And thanks to Aoife, he had the ability to keep from tearing down his mate's ambitions but to build up something more sustainable for himself.

"First up," he said, "I've two more legs of my trip to finish. Okinawa and the Whitsundays."

"Right." Greg's tone stiffened. "Have you seen Sam's bucket-list wall?"

"*Dad...*"

"Bucket-list wall?" Kellan asked.

Greg's gaze darted between his son and Kellan. He backed up a step. "Excuse me for now. I, uh, see a friend I need to catch up with."

"Wait," Kellan said to Sam as they watched Greg make his way painstakingly across the room. "You mean the pictures and maps in the shop office? Those are places you want to go? I assumed it was all places you'd been."

Sam's mouth flattened. "The pictures are places I've been. The maps were for future travel."

Were. Oh, Sam. "It's like my list."

"Not nearly as important," Sam said.

"Don't even try to tell me it doesn't bother you to have something unfinished like that."

"It's not unfinished. It was just inspiration. Sometimes other things get in the way. My diving buddy's been a little busy recovering from a car accident, you know?" His eyes flashed green fire.

"Maybe it's time to take Franci or Archer along, if your dad isn't keen on going." *Or me.*

"Can we talk about this later?" A snap, one that turned heads, including Rachel's.

Kellan cringed. Not the kind of attention he'd been aiming for this evening. He held up his glass. "A toast! To Rachel! She keeps us well fed, well loved and well informed."

She lifted her own champagne flute. "And to Kellan! If only you could stick around."

He had some definite thoughts on how he could make that happen. It warmed him to know Rachel liked the idea. Picturing having a home here was easy, being a part of this overflowing circle of friends.

Family.

"You're too kind, love." He tipped his glass in her direction and winked. His plans, still tender and new, unfurled inside him like the spirals of the fiddleheads he'd used for tonight's tapenade. Full of possibility and freshness, the promise of growing into something rooted and flourishing. He'd make calls in the morning. Start investigating business possibilities here.

But with Sam's hesitation about relationships,

going from something long distance and loose to Kellan following his heart back to Oyster Island after he finished his list would require some finessing.

"I'm serious, honey. This better not be the last we see of you," Rachel said, joining him and Sam after the crowd returned their attention to their own conversations.

"I'm hoping it isn't, either."

You'll need to sell Sam on that, not me.

Chapter Thirteen

An oversized clock with quarter hands that marked the time in fifteen-second intervals, the kind often found at a swimming pool, hung on the wall of Sam's shop. He'd liked the multicolored numbers and had picked it up at a yard sale on the mainland when he was outfitting Otter Marine Tours with racks and shelving.

Today, he sat behind the counter with his scheduling binder, feeling like the second hands were twirling against his body.

He'd woken up, hoping to enjoy one of his last few mornings with Kell, but the bed had been empty. He'd walked out to a living area drenched in intense focus. Papers and charts covered the island and dining table—sketches of dishes and menus, lists of ingredients, financial projections, all written in Kell's bold script. By the looks of it, Kell had been brain-storming new dishes and possibilities based on some of the ingredients he'd been foraging on Oyster Island. Sam didn't know how that was going to fit into an Irish fine dining angle, but he had no doubt Kell could make it happen.

It was nice, really, knowing that their hikes and dives had inspired something new, even though it was going to be downright impossible to build anything themselves. Yeah, he was going to try. And he'd enjoy the long-distance love while it lasted. But who were they kidding? It would be too hard to keep it going forever. How often would they really be able to see each other? And communicating over phones and computers would only fulfill for so long.

He'd left the apartment with a sweet kiss and had ripped home to change.

While there, he'd gotten an email from Charlotte's math teacher. When he'd told his dad about it and mentioned that it would be nice to shift Charlotte's school communications back to Greg, his dad had agreed.

One fewer thing on Sam's plate, something that might help mend his relationship with his younger sister, too.

Still, it didn't free Sam up to be in London as much as would be necessary to keep a relationship together.

The big clock's second hand ticked away, reminding him of their dwindling time together.

It also reminded him that Franci was late again.

His gut twinged. She was supposed to take a small

tour group out in the zodiac today, and she usually was prompter when she had paying guests waiting for her, especially with all the schedule juggling Sam had been doing these past weeks to accommodate her request not to dive. Why the hell was she acting so weird? On the outside, she was her normal sunshine self, but every so often an uncharacteristically dark cloud poked through.

"Sam, man, that clock doesn't hold the secrets to the universe," Archer said dryly, petting his dog and checking over the client list for the dive trip he and Nic were operating today. Sam would be left alone with prepping the monthly records for the accountant and watching over Honu. Maybe Kell would be able to take a break from his own paperwork. There was still so much of Oyster Island Sam wanted to share before he lost his chance. They could take the Labrador out for a hike along the North Ring trail.

But if Franci didn't show up, he'd have all sorts of problems to deal with. He crossed his arms. "I'm worried about my sister."

Archer grunted, mouth firming into a line.

"The hell does that mean?"

His friend shook his head. "Go get a coffee or something. Get me one, too. I'll manage any walk-ins. And she'll be here. She always eventually shows."

"What do you know? Should I be worried?"

Archer was a blank wall. "The coffee, Sam."

He grumbled his way over to Hideaway Bakery.

Winnie was behind the counter when he blew through the door.

His mom stood in the corner next to a rack of mugs for sale, embracing someone wearing a beanie and a thick sweater.

Wait, not just someone. Franci.

At least he knew where she was. It was a "ran in to get a coffee and lost track of time" day, not "I woke up feeling like I ruined my dad's life and can't get out of the covers."

Sam let out a relieved breath. "Franci! Check the time!" he said as he lined up to order his latte and Archer's usual double-shot Americano with a splash of oat milk. "Want me to add a chai to my order?"

Franci poked her head from behind Rachel. She smeared a hand across her damp eyes. "No, thanks."

Taking in his sister's tears, Sam straightened. Crap. Crying, twice in a month?

She'd asked him not to push, but it was so damn hard not to. Why wasn't she willing to lean on him?

Gentling what he knew was a frown to a smile, he beckoned to her with a hand.

She bit her lip and sent Rachel a wary glance.

With his mom's back to him, Sam couldn't hear her reply or see what was on her face, but she squeezed Franci's shoulder.

His neck tingled with suspicion. What was he missing, here? He forced himself to take a deep breath.

She trudged in his direction and came right up to him, resting her forehead on his chest. "Hey."

Ringing his arms around her back, he squeezed. "Rough morning?"

"What gave it away?"

"We all have them. But you're upset, and just as Dad's starting to turn a corner, make a bunch of progress... I'd hoped we'd all benefit from that."

She snorted. "You're predictable, Sammy."

"Huh?"

One of the cashiers from the grocery store stood behind them in the line, tapping her toe and glaring. Not every local embodied the island spirit. Raising a brow, Sam jerked his head for her to pass and gave Franci a squeeze.

"Unlike you," she said, "not everything in my life revolves around Dad."

"Hey, that's an exaggeration."

Shifting her head to rest her cheek over the logo on his zippered work jacket, she said, "I guess Charlotte and I take up a bunch of your brain space, too."

"Because I love you all. But I'm going to work on it, I promise—"

She lifted her head, eyes wide. "Do you have room to love another family member?"

"Huh? Are you seeing someone or something?"

"No." Fear swam in her eyes. "I'm pregnant."

It was just a whisper. No one else would have been able to hear it.

Even so, all the sound in the shop stopped.

Wait, no. People kept on drinking their coffee and laughing. He could see them moving, ignoring how Franci had just announced something that would change the fabric of their family. It was his ears that had stopped working, the clinks and clatters of mugs and cutlery and the hum of conversation muffled by a constant ringing.

"That is…" His voice sounded echoey. "Not exactly a small thing, Francine!"

"It's literally microscopic."

"It's literally *monumental*." A baby. Eventually, anyway. Just a sparkle now, considering Franci wasn't showing.

"It's literally something you might want to talk about somewhere that isn't the coffee line," his mom said, kissing both their cheeks as she passed them to scoot behind the counter. "Here, have a cookie. Both of you." She passed over two salad-plate-sized chocolate chip cookies tucked in paper bags. "Go outside and let the breeze blow away your stresses."

He was agog. "I don't think the breeze can—"

"One day at a time, honey," Rachel said to Franci, both ignoring and cutting Sam off. "Whatever you need, it's yours."

Franci nodded, then grabbed Sam's arm with a mittened hand and pulled him toward the back door.

Once they were alone and leaning on the railing, he managed a breath. Wind blew in his ears, making the incessant buzzing fade. "Holy God, Franci. That's why Archer's been covering your shifts. He knows." His friend brushing the Cheezie dust off Franci's mouth popped into his head, and his pulse leaped. "Wait, is he—"

"*No.* Absolutely not. He was just the first to notice." She was pale. "I can't dive anymore, Sam. I already did, though, before I realized what was happening. What if that caused harm? I haven't been able to see a doctor yet. Some of the websites—"

"You know better than to let a web search diagnose things," he said quietly.

"I know, I know, but I wasn't able to get an appointment right away. And as soon as you see 'decompression disease' you can't unsee it. I considered an abortion, really. Not because of the diving, because every option's been running through my head. I'll be alone—the father is out of state and wants nothing to do with raising a child. I contacted him. But I decided… I just knew…"

She held a mittened fist to her mouth and whimpered.

"Fran," Sam said. Tears swam in her eyes. He caught one as it slid down her pale cheek. "Happy tears, or sad ones?"

She took a deep breath. "Happy. I want to be a mom, Sam. We have the best family, and after the car accident… After not being able to stop it and Dad's still hurting and you're tied in knots all the time and I want to bring something good into our lives for a change. And what's better than a baby? I know if this pregnancy ends up being viable, I'll be ready. I have so much love—" Her voice cracked. "So much love to give."

Her words cascaded around him like a rain shower, some falling on the ground without touching him, some spattering him in the face, prickling and sharp. "Franci, you're not alone. Never. And for Christ's sake, the accident wasn't your fault. There was no way you could have prevented it."

"I know."

Wiping a hand down his face, he said, "How are you feeling?"

"Sick," she groused.

"I'm sorry." He rubbed her back. "Does Dad know?"

She nodded. "And my mom, though she managed to make it about herself, as always. And your mom and Winnie, obviously—I needed to assure them I wasn't sick with a bug after handling their food yesterday. Charlotte doesn't. I'd better tell her today, in case someone heard in the coffee shop. I should probably be more careful about it, keep the news to myself since it's still early and I could miscarry, but everyone's going to notice I'm not diving. You'll need to hire someone new. And I wouldn't hide a miscarriage from the world, anyway, so…"

Eyes glistening, she covered her mouth with a hand and whimpered.

"Hey." He pulled her close. "Big news, I know. You don't need to figure it all out today. And when it comes to the shop, I've got that under control."

Though losing a dive leader for a year or so would be tricky, especially if he was looking to take time off to visit Kell.

That was his problem, though, not hers. "You don't need to figure it all out today," she echoed with a watery wink.

No, he didn't. He needed to figure out *some* things ASAP, though.

His business, a new family member—or for now, at least, a sister who needed more support than normal—he tried to line that up with what he'd been planning with Kell and didn't see a way to square the equation.

"I have a doctor's appointment on Saturday at two."

Exactly when he had Kell's last two dives booked, based on the tides. "Do you have someone going with you?"

She shook her head.

"Do you want company?"

A nod. "Please. Especially with the diving thing. The nitrogen. Having someone who understands the science behind it…"

"Okay. I'll make it work." He could switch Kellan to the group test on the same day.

"Let's go talk to Arch. We'll figure out today first."

They made their way to the shop and found Archer and Nic processing the first few dive clients.

"No coffee?" Archer asked mildly.

"Have a cookie instead." Handing him the small paper bag, Sam jerked his head at his employee. Arch followed him silently into the office.

"I'm going to need to switch any of your ecotours for Franci's dives on an ongoing basis. Going to talk to Nic about increasing his hours, too," he said without ceremony.

Archer nodded. "Good. She finally told you."

Sam's ears started ringing again. "She didn't need to keep it from me. I can't believe you figured it out."

"I recognized the signs, having seen my own sister's pregnancies." Archer's face darkened. "And I can count, and if Francine needs me to, I'm happy to take a trip to Boise to straighten out that asshole she was involved with."

She poked her head through the doorway. "Stay out of it, Archer."

He lifted a brow at her and grunted.

"Seriously," she said before disappearing.

Sam inhaled deeply, pushing away his own caveman responses. "She'll let us know what she needs. What I need is to know you don't mind working more."

"We'll all take our turns. Probably need someone else, though, right?"

Sam nodded.

"A friend of mine, a retired coastie living in SoCal, might be interested in filling in for a few months."

"That could be helpful."

"I'll give her a call if you want," Archer said.

What Sam really wanted was to put his head in Kellan's lap and let those rough chef's fingers stroke away his burgeoning headache.

But why should he learn to rely on that when he wouldn't have it all the time?

He needed to keep some space between them.

He was resolved to do just that when Kellan strolled into the otherwise empty shop a couple of hours later.

His gaze latched onto Sam's and his eyebrows knitted together. "What's wrong?"

"I wouldn't say wrong, exactly."

"Lies." Kellan came up to Sam and kissed him, long and slow.

God, how had this man become so vital to Sam's existence in such a short time? Sam had been so stupid, letting himself fall in—

No. Not that.

His lips and tongue tangled with Kell's and he fought to keep his thoughts clear. He hadn't fallen that much. A little, maybe. Kell was magnetic. Who wouldn't want to get bowled over by kisses like these on the regular, coaxed closer with talented hands? The heat in his veins settled in his groin and it was a damn good thing they were alone in the store.

Lust. This was lust.

But the feeling of being a half of a whole? That's love.

"Everyone's out on tours," Sam said, smoothing back the hair that he'd tousled on Kell's head. "I can't take a lunch break."

"No bother. I've a couple more calls I need to make, anyway. But tell me what's on your mind before someone comes in needing your help."

"What makes you think something's on my mind?"

"This." Kell rubbed the spot between Sam's eyebrows. "And these." The corners of his mouth. "And this." A hand over the center of Sam's chest. "I can just feel it, a chroí. It's like we're layers of puff pastry, and someone rolled us together with my gran's giant pin, and now I can't tell what's you and what's me. So yeah, I can tell you're out of sorts."

"Franci's having a baby."

Kell blinked. "*Oh*."

"At least, she hopes to. It's early yet." He covered Kell's hand, still resting in the middle of his chest, with his own. "Might be an uncle come late fall."

"And wouldn't that be a thing."

Ting. Emotions choked the word.

Big ones, considering it was Sam's sister who was knocked up, not Kell's. *Oh. Wait.*

"Thinking of Aoife?" Sam asked gently.

"Sure."

It came out too quick to believe it was wholly true.

He waited for Kell to say more.

Kell only sighed.

"Is it wrong of me to be thankful it's not Charlotte?" Sam asked.

"No." Kell let out another long breath. "I can't imagine being seventeen and dealing with parenthood."

"Franci's only twenty-four."

"She knows herself, though, Sam. She's got a place here."

"That's true." He brushed a hand along Kell's cheek. "Can I ask you a favor? I need to switch you to the group test. It's the same day we were doing the private dive. Arch and Nic are leading it."

Kell withdrew. "Why?"

"I think you'll be better off diving with someone who's not me."

"What?"

"I won't be there with you in Okinawa and Australia, and you'll want to know that you'll be comfortable working with another partner. I'll refund the extra cost."

Which was all true.

"Hey." Kell crossed his arms. "What's *really* going on?"

Crap. He owed this man honesty. "Franci has her first doctor's appointment. She's worried about some diving-specific things. I want to be there for her."

The face Sam was so quickly growing to love the most fell. "You could've led with that."

"I…"

"Seriously. Do you think I wouldn't understand? This isn't an everyday change. I get it."

"Even so, I'm letting you down." Sam could want to meet Kellan halfway, but he sure as hell wasn't putting it in motion. He knew that. And it hurt to fail so early on.

"Not the way you think." Kell's gaze darted to the side. "The schedule change is an annoyance at best. But you not communicating with me, not trusting me to be reasonable—*that* concerns me."

"I'm sorry."

"I am, too." Kell shook his head. "I need to get to my Zoom call."

The distance was probably a good thing. It was all they'd have, come next week.

Kellan surfaced at the end of his second dive on Saturday, next to his diving partner. A partner who was specifically *not* Sam.

The young woman, Tracy, a Friday Harbor resident

who'd hopped islands to complete her certification, beamed at him. "We did it!"

"Good job." He didn't have it in him to match her bright smile. Where was the sense of accomplishment he'd expected?

Archer emerged from the depths with an eruption of bubbles. He immediately narrowed in on Kellan. "You okay?"

"You know, I am." A lump formed in his throat, and more than salt water stung the corners of his eyes.

"This month has been a long haul for you."

"Worth it, though." And it felt wrong that Sam wasn't here for the final step.

He itched to get back to Hideaway Wharf.

The half hour it took for the seven students to get back on the boat, out of their gear, dried off and in warm-up clothes felt like a whole day.

Kellan sat to the side as the rest of the chatty, jovial gang celebrated their certifications on their way into the dock.

The coastline was so familiar now—the shape of the tree line above the cliffs, gulls sunning on rocks jutting out into the water. The boat rounded the east point and the docks came into view. Cars were loading onto the ferry.

That'll be me tomorrow.

But it wouldn't be the end. He was coming back. He'd completed his dives. Rory had even cooled off enough to make peace with Kellan's ultimate decision to just be an investor in Aisling instead of being the executive chef, which meant he had something more definitive to tell Sam. Sure, he'd been angry the other day when Sam had skirted around the truth of the rescheduling. He'd also known that he wasn't being entirely forthcoming, either. They were still new at this, at finding a balance between togetherness and independence, at meeting previous commitments and having the guts to make new ones.

The colors of the waterfront buildings reflected on the water. Patches of cyan and yellow, violet and seafoam. And the pinkest house on Oyster Island, the one with the apartment on the second floor.

He'd be thinking of it as home, if he wasn't careful.

He checked his texts. Multiple message notifications cascaded in a list.

Rory: Steven is accusing me of still sulking. I'm not. Good luck on the dive today. Let me know how it goes.

Matias: Come by for a beer after your dive. IOU after the snack mix you made me.

Unknown Number: This is Rachel. You've got this, honey.

Nothing from Sam. His heart sank, and he was about to jam his mobile in his jacket pocket when it buzzed.

Sam: Franci's appt was fine. Dr isn't worried about her diving.

A relief. Kellan had been worried about her. Another buzz.

Sam: Proud of you no matter what. How did it go?

Kellan put his cell away. Sam could wait a few more minutes to find out.

The boat slowed. His excitement finally started to build. He'd *done it.* He'd be able to fulfill his promise to Aoife, in so many more ways than he'd intended. The dive cert, the rest of his list—small things in comparison to falling in love and changing his business plan.

A burly shadow came out from behind the supply hut at the end of the pier and jogged down the ramp toward the *Oyster Queen*'s slip. The second Archer pulled the boat in, Sam launched over the side and pulled Kell to his feet with both hands.

"It's okay. You can try again. I know you need to be on the one o'clock ferry, but we can go out first thing, knock off whatever skill tripped you up—"

"Sam, stop." Kell kissed his boyfriend until he felt Sam's shoulders relax under his jacket. "Why are you assuming I failed?"

"You didn't reply right away. I figured that meant you'd run into problems."

"No." He cupped Sam's cheeks. "It meant I wanted to tell you in person. And to say thank you."

"You did it?" Strapping arms lifted Kellan off his feet.

Screw a pink apartment.

This was home.

He nuzzled deeper into Sam's embrace and completely lost the ability to keep his thoughts to himself. A buzz of activity surrounded them, all Kellan's test mates unloading their things and chattering happily. He faintly heard Tracy shouting a goodbye to him and waved in response, but couldn't take his eyes off the man holding him like a most precious thing.

"I'm falling in love with you," he confessed.

Sam's eyes widened, clear, sincere. Nervous, absolutely. He bit his lip.

Kellan's heart was revving as fast as the boat's engine at full bore. "No need to respond in kind. Promise. It's meant to be a gift, not a burden."

"You are absolutely a gift, Kellan Murphy. And you deserve to hear the same from me."

So say it. Please. "Not until you know it's true."

"It's…it's something. You have become someone so important to me. It's overwhelming. And I'm terrified of making a mistake, and also terrified to lose you—"

"You've just found me. You're not going to lose me."

"You're leaving tomorrow," Sam whispered, his lips teasing the skin behind Kellan's ear.

Kellan's knees wobbled. Sam's declaration wasn't exactly the words his heart craved to hear, but they were honest and meaningful. "Only in body."

He would absolutely be leaving his heart behind.

Kellan pressed his lips to the fluttering pulse on Sam's neck.

Sam's breath hitched.

"You know," Archer said, his words invading Kellan's cocoon of comforting arms and overwhelming feelings, "the two of you are cute and all, but you could pick a better time to make out on the deck of the *Queen*. Like, say, after we've cleaned up."

Sam flipped his friend the middle finger without looking at him. "After I help Archer, I want to take you out to celebrate."

Kellan tried to look excited about the prospect. "If you want."

"What?"

"It's my last night here for a while."

Sam's face clouded and he rocked back on his heels. "Don't remind me."

"I'm feeling selfish. I want you to myself."

A slow grin split Sam's face. "Let's celebrate in, then."

They cleaned up in record time and before Kellan knew it, Sam was dragging him up the stairs to the flat. "Quick, get inside before someone can interrupt us."

Kellan laughed and opened the door.

The door slammed. Strong hands shoved Kellan against the wood, laden with the urgency of someone who knew they were getting their last sips and tastes. Frantic lips moved over his mouth, his neck. Sam lifted Kellan's hands, kissed his palms, then held them tight.

Kellan tightened his fingers around Sam's. "A

mhuirnín. We've got hours yet. And then…as much time as we want."

"Um, the opposite, really."

Lips nibbled at the skin exposed by the loose V-neck of Kell's T-shirt. Mother of God, he was going to lose his head if Sam kept doing that, and then they'd be naked and shagging and would never get around to talking.

"Not when I move here." Desperation launched the words past any lingering worries.

Sam stumbled back, only stopping when he bumped into the kitchen stool Kell had neglected to tuck under the island. The stool tipped and crashed to the floor.

Sam left it and gripped the countertop. "*When*."

An echo, not a question.

"Yes. When."

Sam's cheeks paled.

Kellan's stomach twisted. He was glad to be leaning against the door so it could take his weight. "Not the exact reaction I'd hoped for."

"Sweetheart. I—No, it—"

"Still not ideal."

Sam rubbed his hands over his face.

Crossing his arms over his chest, Kellan slid down to sit on the hardwood floor. "You can be honest. I can take it."

A stumbling step, and Sam was kneeling next to Kellan, holding his hands, mouth twisted and gaping. "You don't want to move here. Not really. After living in London? You'll get bored."

"That's your experience talking, not mine."

"You're a city boy. The Oyster Island annual Christmas play and the occasional high school soccer game can't live up to all the things you were talking about with my dad the other night."

"I spent my summers in a seaside village, Sam. I know what I'm getting into," Kellan said, a testy edge creeping into his tone. "I love it here. I've never felt like I do here, like I can just...*be*. I finally got through to Rory, got him to understand what I needed. He's disappointed, but gets it. I'm going to invest in Aisling and have a little left over to build a business here."

"What business?" Sam's voice was raw.

"Either a place of my own or a partnership. I'll have enough of a cushion that I can explore my options without panicking."

He wasn't panicking, anyway.

Sam seemed to be. White flared around his irises. "I can't ask you to compromise like that. I... I asked Alyssa to stay. And she grew to hate it. Hate being married to me. I can't—" his words were raw with regret "—I can't ask *you* to stay, and then have you grow to hate it, too."

"You're not asking," Kellan said gently. "I'm offering."

Sam stood, started to pace. "But what do I have to offer? With Franci being pregnant... The tour schedule is going to drastically change with her unable to dive. So many changes in staffing. I'll be working more, and things with my dad are easing up a little but not entirely, and—" Sam let out a strangled sound and then swore. "But that's an excuse."

"Sure and it is." Kellan rose, went over to the counter and leaned on it. "I mean, at least you can see that. We both know this isn't about Francine." The truth welled in his chest, damping down the heat from their kiss. "Though I don't want to minimize the change for you. It's not just to your staffing, it's to your family."

A deep yearning pulled at him. What he'd do to be a part of that family.

"I have to be here for it all," Sam said. "But it's too much to ask of you."

"Again, *you're not* asking."

"I know," Sam croaked. "And it still scares me."

Kellan could see that in each wide-eyed blink, in the slump of Sam's shoulders.

"A relationship can't survive without trust," he said. He'd worked for so long to believe he was worthy of love, and it was taking everything he could to keep believing that the barrier wasn't his own inherent shortcomings but the cascade effect of Sam being betrayed. Was it a fool's mission to build a business on the island, not knowing for certain if Sam would come around?

When Sam finally said something, his voice was a raspy mess. "You don't think I trust you."

"You don't yet. Not really," Kellan said. "I'd love to show you that you can, though."

"I wish I wasn't so much work for you."

"Relationships are *always* work. Look at how much you put into caring for your family." Kellan wouldn't

say it was too much—it wasn't for him to decide—
but he could take care of Sam for once. Linking hands
with the man who held his heart, he led the way to the
bedroom. "You've built your life around being needed,
around doing the caring. And the most important time
you let yourself be vulnerable, with the person you
chose to marry, it was with someone who didn't end
up needing you *or* taking care of you."

Gingerly reclining against the pillows, Sam opened
an arm wide.

Kellan shook his head. "Everyone assumes you're
the caretaker. The big, brawny spoon." He spread
Sam's legs and knelt between them, bracketing his
hands on the pillow and dropping small but potent
kisses. In all the times they'd been that intimate, Sam
had always topped. But Kellan remembered he'd said
he was open to other positions. "Add in the fact you
were married to a cis woman—I bet a few blokes have
assumed you don't like bottoming."

"That's happened more than once," Sam admitted.

"And I bet you don't insist on getting your turn."

"Not often, no."

"A shame." Kellan lay belly down between Sam's
legs, a thick thigh on either side of his hips, the hard-
ening bulge under Sam's jeans rubbing his own.

"We were…we were talking about trust. That's
important." Sam's fingers gripped Kellan's arse and
pulled him even closer. "Don't want to get distracted."

"I've said what I've needed to say." He tugged
Sam's shirt off and laid a row of kisses along bared

collarbones. Those pecs, the broad chest and solid waist below... *Unfh*.

"And I didn't answer the way you wanted."

"Yet." He drifted his mouth over hard planes and soft, hair-dusted skin. "Best way to build trust is through action, though."

"This kind of action?" Sam gasped and lifted his hips as Kellan ran his tongue along his lower belly.

"In part, yes." Kellan undid Sam's belt and fly, then kissed the damp spot on the underwear below, the rigid, leaking tip. "I want to show you I'm falling in love with you." He sneaked his fingers through gaping jeans and slowly rubbed Sam's jutting erection. "Partly with an excellent goodbye. And partly by keeping my promise to return. I'll come back for you. And for me. For my mental health and my sense of balance and the fact I've found a community here that feels like home for the first time since my gran's place in Youghal."

Sam groaned. "Might have caught all that? But your hand is kind of perfect and..."

He scooted the jeans down a bit more and followed with his hand. The thin underwear didn't provide much of a barrier, and he pressed a fingertip to the tight entrance below.

Sam let out a guttural plea.

God, Kellan loved making a big, strapping man lose control. Making *Sam* lose control. And he'd do pretty much anything to have his erection nudging Sam's arse instead of his finger. His body clamored to be closer. "Can I top you, Sam?"

"You'd better."

Sam went to roll over but Kellan stopped him with a firm hand to the shoulder.

"This way. Face-to-face."

And thank God Sam agreed, because Kellan couldn't get enough of every flash of pleasure, of yearning. The grin he earned stripping Sam, and then himself, naked. The fluttering eyelids and catch of breath, deepening to a moan the more he prepped and stretched Sam.

"Relax, a chroí," Kellan said, working his fingers slowly, leaning up to taste Sam's lips. Salty, still, maybe from Kellan's own skin and hair. "We're not in a hurry."

"You might not be. I'm dying."

"Ah, but are you *ready* and dying?"

He'd not joked around with that word in a while. It felt good.

Better than good. The world blurred, all spicy man smell and soft sheets and a well-built body under him.

Need knotted at the base of his spine. What could top Sam's strong fingers slicking a condom down his length, of thrusting, first gentle, then fast, into the man he was falling for?

Him believing I'll still want this a year, a decade, a lifetime from now.

He thrust again, grinning at Sam arching below him, hissing at the fingers that dug into his shoulders.

Focus on now. Forever will come.

Now. Yes. This moment. Sam, vulnerable and trusting him to take him over the edge.

The future would come. And to get there, it would be one precious moment at a time. And hopefully many, many more nights like tonight, when he got to wreck Sam Walker.

Chapter Fourteen

"You ruined me," Sam mumbled, squinting against the morning light streaming through the curtains they'd forgotten to close after they'd taken a shower together last night. He pulled the sheets over them both, feeling every one of his body's post-sex twinges and aches.

He flipping loved it.

Kell snuggled close. Fabric rasped Sam's naked body, a soft T-shirt and a pair of those lounge pants that looked like brunch wear.

"Wait, you're dressed. When did you get dressed?" he said, the just-woken fog clearing with every blink.

"I'm after popping to your mum's for cinnamon buns, coffees and a goodbye."

"You did that without me noticing?" Sulking, he made a face.

"I brought them back. They're in the kitchen."

Now that Kell mentioned it, just enough cinnamon aroma clung to his shirt to recognize.

Sam buried his nose and inhaled the comforting smell. The aroma of gooey pastries, the clean, peppery spice that was Kell's alone.

Looping his arms around the man, he sighed. "I want to bottle you."

"No need. I'll let you know the second my return flight is booked."

He stared into bottomless gray eyes, searching for any hint that Kell was having second thoughts about his wild plan.

They were bright with confidence.

With love.

Sam's heart flipped. This man was worth letting the words out. "I *am* falling for you. In case it wasn't clear."

"I know y'are. And it was." His hands were so gentle, stroking Sam's hair back from his forehead. "That's why this is worth pursuing."

It was, but it wasn't that easy. The flip went tight, clenching until his whole abdomen roiled. "Kellan…"

"What?"

"You've had a big loss. Is now really the time to be making life-changing decisions? Do you really know what you want? Or am I a good balm for your wounds?"

Kellan sat up, mouth going slack. "You can't be serious."

"One of us has to be."

"You're putting this on *me*? When it's your trust issue that's raking up all these questions?"

"I can't deny that." Sam sat up, too, tucking the sheet around his waist. Talk about being literally and figuratively naked. The skin crawled on his back, cold prickles from being exposed. "But I'm worried you're focusing on my issues to avoid looking at your own."

"All I've done is look at me, since I got here. I went from not wanting to be in a boat on that water to being okay cavorting with seals! I slowed down enough to recognize it was a necessary change, and that it was something I'd never be able to do in London. And everyone accepted me. And I started to see places I'd fit—including this bed—and I loved that possibility. So why shouldn't I settle here? It's not like there's anywh-wh-where else…" A sob broke from his chest. "Or any-anyone else…"

Sam watched the grief crack through the happy persona Kellan had constructed to keep himself upright.

Waves of pain, of loss, twisting and barreling out in great sobs.

Sam held him, absorbing the agony of a man who didn't have many arms to hold him. And he wanted to be this for Kell, a safe harbor, a resting place.

They lay back down, Kell's tears slick on Sam's chest. A pile of Kleenexes grew.

"I'm sorry," Kell finally said, choking in a breath. "That was…"

"Necessary." Sam cupped soft curls at the back of Kell's skull and hugged tight.

"I suppose, but it's giving you the wrong impression." He rose on an elbow and waved a hand, indicating his face. "I'm not normally a holy show."

That had to mean *mess*. "Part of you is."

Pink splotched Kell's cheeks. "Excuse me?"

"It's okay that you are. Who wouldn't be?" Sam made a face. "But I don't think you're acknowledging the possibilities enough, here. A massive change like you're suggesting... If it doesn't work, if it turns out not to be what you want, then what will you do?"

Kell's jaw hung.

"When you arrived, you were determined to get home and fulfill a lifelong dream. And now you don't want it anymore, and I'm..." If he was going to challenge Kell, he might as well put an honest label on his own emotions. "I'm afraid you'll change your mind. I want to protect you from what my ex went through, and the fallout that hurt all of us."

Kell was so still. That body and mind, so often in constant motion, frozen. "The only person you're protecting is you. I'm coming back. For me. Whether or not we're friends or partners when I do that is up to you."

"And I want to believe it, but I can't."

Wiping a thumb under one eye, then the other, Kell scoffed. "We make our own guarantees, Sam. Life doesn't promise them. We have to go after what we want."

"How am I supposed to live—" Sam's voice cracked "—never...never knowing if the person I love is truly happy? If *you* are truly happy?"

"You'll need to answer that for yourself."

Good. He was getting through. Saving this man from making a risky decision that might not pan out. "I can't let you throw away your life on this island, Kellan."

Kellan snorted. "Bollocks."

"What?"

"I'm not throwing my life away on anything, Sam Walker." Climbing on the bed, he went to the closet and pulled out his giant suitcase. "If anyone's throwing their life away on this island, if anyone's not truly happy, it's you. I know I could live here and build something fulfilling. And if you need to see me do it to believe it, fine. I've some promises to keep and some loose threads to tie, but once that's done, I know where I want to land."

"And what if I can never be who you need me to be?"

Kellan's hand stilled on the zipper of his still-empty suitcase. "I don't know. Something else to ponder while I'm knotting those loose threads, I suppose."

Sam stared at the sheets, unable to keep his gaze locked with the brimming hurt in Kell's. His chest throbbed.

Do you want a little pain now, or a lot later?

He didn't want pain at all. He wanted to wake up tomorrow and have this man in his bed, and to believe that would still be the case a year from now. A decade.

That lifetime Kell had mentioned.

He just didn't believe it was possible.

"I'll work on it." Sam lifted his head, caught the spark of hope in Kell's eyes.

"I will, too."

"Too many people haven't loved you like you deserve, Kellan. I want to learn *not* to be one of those people," Sam vowed. "If I can."

Kellan emptied an armful of socks and underwear into his suitcase, followed by a stack of T-shirts, including a familiar-looking navy one on top.

The undershirt Sam had been wearing under his button-up last night.

Kell must have snuck it into his packing when Sam wasn't looking.

Sam's heart broke a little further.

"If it makes a difference," Kell said, hands stilling around a stack of sweatpants, "I believe you can. Do you need space while I'm gone, or constant contact?"

"Surprise me."

Surprise me.

The challenge kept his impatience at bay. Kept him from thinking too much about Sam's worries. *What if I can never be who you need me to be?*

Kellan had built up a vision in his head, one so easy to construct, of finding work or starting a business on the island. Of finding family there. Of being with Sam. A tripod of sorts. Would it still stand if one of the legs came off?

Unable to answer that question, he spent a couple of food-filled nights in Tokyo with an old friend from cooking school. Thought of Sam while eating crab and anago and the most delicate chawanmushi he'd ever had on his tongue.

He posted a fleet of pictures to Instagram. Lying in bed one of the nights, wearing Sam's undershirt, he saw the little Otter Marine Tours icon in the people who'd watched his jam-packed story and the reel of his top-ten eats in Tokyo.

So he'd intrigued Sam. But what would surprise him?

He didn't know.

While he brainstormed options, he kept any direct contact with Sam to texts about his itinerary. Nothing personal. Just enough for Sam to know he was safe.

He'd arrived. Was in his hotel. Paid an exorbitant fee to change his flights to Okinawa—he couldn't resist a two-day jaunt to Kyoto to see cherry blossoms since he'd missed the mid-March bloom in Tokyo. Probably should be conserving his money given he wasn't certain what work would look like when he got back to Oyster Island, but how often would he be in Japan?

The ache to share all these things with Sam was close to spilling out of his chest, but it felt right not to release a gush of photos and feelings via a messaging app. They both needed some space after that breakdown he'd had the other day, and after Sam's ugly spill of doubts.

He woke up the fifth morning and was about to text his flight times when the WhatsApp icon lured him in.

His hair was a right shambles and pillow marks

lined his face, but that didn't matter. God knew he'd give anything to have Sam's own mussed hair and pillow-lined cheek in bed next to him.

He pressed record. "I love you. Surprise."

Before he could second-guess himself, he pressed send. *Ugh.* As if that little clip was enough, or anything new and exciting.

Pressing record again, he said, "I'm rubbish at surprises, apparently, because you had to have known that." He jammed his free hand in his hair. "I miss you." He flashed the camera at the empty pillow next to him. "It'd be a squish, but you being right there would make it better, like."

Send.

He spent the whole trip to the airport and his flight regretting his show of cringe.

An alert buzzed on his mobile the second he took it off airplane mode and connected to the Okinawa airport Wi-Fi.

Two video replies. Sam, against navy blue sheets, a sleepy look in his eye. "I'll always be surprised when you tell me you love me." He frowned. "Should probably work on that. God, my counselor's going to be able to go to Bora Bora for Christmas from my fees alone." A rueful smile. "Be safe, sweetheart."

And the second: "I love you, too."

Holy sainted Mother. He *what*? And he'd confessed it in a recording?

Though—side benefit of that—Kellan would be able to watch it on repeat until they saw each other again.

Waiting at the luggage carousel, he glanced up at the ceiling. "Your itinerary was too long, Aoife, love. But I'll do it."

She'd picked him a paradise, she had, down to the hotel and dive boat reservations booked by her executor, and he was hardly able to enjoy it. Where was she leading him?

Later that afternoon, he walked for miles up and down the beaches, contemplating his next steps, the surf erasing his footprints with gentle waves. The water was a thousand shades of turquoise, the sand a pale, glittering almond.

When he returned to his room, Aoife's note waited for him with a bottle of sake and two cups.

Pinching the bridge of his nose and pouring them each a glass, he sliced open the envelope.

My precious eejit—
You deserved an easy one after the wolf eels.
    I wish I was there to see if you did it.
    No, that's not quite right.
    I'll figure out a way to be there.
    And I know you did it.
    Soak up the lazy days. I'm putting you to work in Australia.
—A

He tossed back one of the drinks. Not the respectful way to consume a fine beverage, but it'd been a long day. "You already put me to work. But I'll do more, if it means getting Sam."

Sitting on the edge of the bed, he idly stroked the cool cotton duvet cover. *What if I never get Sam? Will I still want to be there?*

It was a trust issue.

And I need to trust myself.

"I was happy there," he said to his shoes.

A squawk came from outside the window. A smug-looking gull, perched on the rail of the Juliet balcony. It pecked at the window.

"Seriously? Another seagull?"

Peck, peck.

He toasted the seagull with the second cup of sake and downed it. He wasn't going to spend his life living for his sister, doing things she wouldn't be able to do herself. But he wasn't going to forget that each day was an opportunity, and he was fortunate to be living in this moment. Not everyone got the time they needed to do the things they wanted.

Nor did they get the time to *decide* exactly what it was they wanted.

He had so many blessings, and Oyster Island had been rife with more.

Sam or no Sam, he'd found a place there where his nerves weren't ragged and his days weren't harried.

The seagull stared at him. He swore the creature narrowed its eyes.

"I know, I know. I'll be pure miserable if Sam and I end up friends instead. But that doesn't mean I wouldn't want to live there."

He'd rather build something in a community he'd

come to love rather than go back to a life of lonely stress.

With something approaching a satisfied nod, the bird flew away.

Chuckling, Kell reached for his laptop satchel. He opened the device. He had an early dive time to make in the morning, but he had an idea, and it couldn't wait.

Chapter Fifteen

Sam tapped a toe on the bar rail in front of his usual stool and took a long drink of the rotating sour Matias had just brought in.

"It's good," he called to his friend, who was working the taps.

"Your boyfriend picked it out."

"Kahale, I told you—"

"Yeah, yeah." Matias slammed a bowl of snack mix in front of Sam. A few pieces of furikake-glazed Chex cereal and a pretzel stick went flying.

Sam scowled at it. "He made this, too, didn't he?"

"He did. Trying to replicate some Hawaiian recipe Archer was going on about. Took him five batches to get it right."

Sam's chest ached. Kell had put in so much effort to fit in a circle Sam himself often took for granted.

All he wanted right now was to have that generous heart on the stool next to him, telling him about the various tweaks he'd made to the recipe.

Instead, Franci sat beside him, eating a plate of waffle fries and looking slightly green. Palming her stomach, she groaned and pushed the dish away. "Damn it, Mati, I tried."

Matias came over, possessive concern knitting his thick eyebrows. He slid a couple packages of saltines her way and squeezed her fist. "You need to keep something down, Strawberry."

Franci held the back of her hand to her seamed lips and shook her head. "You guys can stop hovering. I want to do this myself."

Sam pushed the hood of her sweatshirt to the side and rubbed between her shoulder blades. "You're not alone, Fran. There's no point in trying to act like you are."

"It's complicated. And hard." She crossed her arms on the bar and rested her forehead on them. "And the ripple effect…"

"Don't worry about that." The stress of his week weighed on his shoulders, though. He'd played so much scheduling Tetris, before posting a job vacancy on a hiring website. Two days later, he'd taken it down when Archer got through to his SoCal friend, who'd jumped on the chance for a few months of dive work. "The new hire will be here at the end of the month."

"Maybe by then Kellan will be back and you'll stop it with the damn frown," Francine mumbled from the cradle of her arms.

"Maybe," Sam said softly. Their communication had been sporadic, and from the pictures he'd seen on social media, Kell was loving Japan. "Or maybe he'll meet someone else and decide subtropical weather is better than Pacific Northwest rain."

"Don't be an ass," Matias snapped. "If your bed's empty once he's done his trip, it'll be your choice, not his."

Sam chucked a small handful of mix into his mouth and chewed, trying not to feel annoyed he hadn't asked Kell to make up a jumbo batch that Sam could serve to hungry divers on their way back to the dock. "Have you been talking to my therapist or something?"

The two appointments he'd had with his counselor since Kell left had left his brain hurting. Turned out divorce came with a package of grief, too, one he'd never properly unwrapped.

Grumbling to himself, Matias ran a cloth over a recently vacated space at the bar. "You're back in therapy? Good."

"Every time I complain about being lonely at night, Dr. Johns agrees with me that it's hard. But then she reminds me I'm alone because I asked for space to think."

"And have you?" Matias asked.

Franci opened a package of crackers without taking her eyes off Sam's face and nibbled on the corner of a saltine.

"Have I what?" Sam asked.

"Thought."

"That's all I've been doing." He took a long drink

of his beer and then winced. His eyes watered from the sour tang.

"I get that," Franci said, saving him from elaborating. "And it sucks, not knowing what to do."

"You meaning the kid, Fran?"

She nodded at Matias. "I was so certain at first, but doubts keep creeping in. I don't know. Is it the right decision? Going through with this?"

"You've gotta answer that for yourself," Matias said.

Familiar, those words. Sam couldn't get them out of his head, crisply enunciated in Kell's accent, punctuated by the pain in his eyes caused by all the doubts Sam had thrown his way.

He didn't know if he could fix that, but he could at least support his sister.

"Whatever you decide, I'm here for you," Sam told her. "Always."

Franci narrowed her eyes. "I hope you don't mean literally being around all the time, Sam. I'm a fully grown adult."

"Yeah, I know."

"Do *not* use me or my pregnancy as an excuse to hide from something good."

"I'm not," he protested.

"You need to see this," Matias said gruffly, plunking his phone on the bar in front of Sam.

A text thread filled the display.

"Isn't this private, man?" Sam asked, uneasy.

"Kellan said I could show you."

Swallowing, Sam took a closer look.

Kellan: Need a sous chef?

Matias: Maybe.

Kellan: I fly back May 13.

Matias: Does Sam know that?

Kellan: He will.

Matias: You really want a sous position?

Kellan: While I figure out something more permanent, sure. And I bet you need someone for the summer.

Matias: You're overqualified.

Kellan: I know, but it would give me time to convince you on this:

The next bubble was only a Word document icon and a file name: *prop....y.doc*.

Sam looked up from the screen, unsure of whether to focus on Kellan having an official return date or having asked Matias for a job. "What's the document?"

"Read it for yourself."

He opened the file and skimmed it. Parts of the brief outline looked familiar. He'd seen those seasonal menu items and profit projections scattered all over the counters in his apartment. He got to the bottom, then stared at Matias. "He wants to be your business partner?"

"Seems so."

Franci bit into a second cracker, eyes wide.

"Do *you* want that?" Sam asked, mind racing. Kell, working across the street from him. Where would he stay? Would he get his own place, or want to live with Sam, or—

Matias waved a hand in front of Sam's face. "Holy hell, man. He has you spinning. And no, I don't want a partnership. I like The Cannery the way it is. I told him he's welcome to my kitchen in the mornings and on the day I'm closed, though. And I'll take him up on his sous chef offer, even though I stand by what I said about him being overqualified."

"How did he sound? Did your refusal of his proposal turn him off?" Jealousy ripped through him. Kell hadn't made any attempts to call him, other than short videos.

"Nah. He started spitballing about what he could do with having the use of a kitchen in the morning. Picnics or a food truck or catering."

"Cooking up foraged food for my tour clients," Sam blurted.

Franci and Matias shared a look.

"Just an idea," Sam explained, feeling embarrassed for some reason.

"Maybe it's not *my* business he needs to work for," Matias said casually. "The guy seems to want to plant roots."

His sister blinked, all innocence. "You love roots, Sammy."

"When they don't get torn up," Sam said.

"He's moving here regardless of you," Matias took an order slip from the person waiting tables tonight and he glanced at it, then lined four cocktail glasses on his silicone spill mat. "Do you want him in your bed, or not?"

"Of course I do," Sam said.

"Then take a step. And if you end up falling on your face, well, I'll pour you a beer and hand you a hanky. You survived the last time you got dumped. Why would another time be different?"

Was it possible for all the eyes of the bar to be on him? Felt like it. He glanced around, making sure no one was watching.

"Because I love him more," he said quietly.

"That's a good thing, don't you think?" Franci said, her cheeks finally getting some pink back in them.

"It might be."

If life was just a series of possibilities linked together with some hope and forward movement, then Sam couldn't ask for a better person to have at his side as he jumped from one *might be* to the next.

He groaned and buried his face in his hands. "I don't think a big enough apology exists for how much I've screwed up."

Franci slid Matias's phone back in front of Sam, an airline website pulled up on the screen. "Wing it, Sammy. Literally."

* * *

Sweat dripped down Kellan's neck as he hauled his suitcase through the door to the rustic resort lobby of his final stop. Fans blew from four directions, ruffling his travel-and-perspiration-wrecked hair—the all-solar-power Whitsundays lodging wasn't air conditioned. It was a tiny place in comparison to anywhere he'd stayed in Japan. Twelve yurts, booked a week at a time, according to the website.

The last two weeks had given him color overload. Kyoto's creamy pink blossoms and the entire blue color gradient of the seas around Okinawa, fish yellower than he knew possible, the rich orange and reds of quail eggs nestled in flying fish roe at his final Japanese dinner. And now the deep, endless black of the star-dotted Whitsunday night sky. Three days of diving, three days of beach cleanup—he'd sleep soundly for once.

That had *not* happened in Japan. The minute he'd tried to rest in a Sam-free bed, he tossed and turned worse than the laundry the time Gran had forgotten to take it off the line during a gale.

Forcing a smile, he sidled up to the check-in desk.

A cheery, Indigenous bloke in his early twenties—Yarran, the name tag read on his tight, resort-issued polo—sized Kellan up. "Our last arrival of the night. Sorry to hear about your flight delays."

Kellan slid his driver's license across the desk. "I could certainly use a beer."

"We have those out on the lawn. Plus a fellow guest or two, if you're feeling like a chinwag. International crowd this week. Some university folks from India, a couple from Johannesburg, a few Americans…"

"And an Irishman with a wicked need for a post-flight shower," he joked.

Sympathy crossed the younger man's face. "Clean up, then a beer?"

"Sure."

Twenty minutes later, he'd dealt with his luggage and washed off at least one layer of travel grime. The last thing he wanted was to chat with people, especially any Americans, except for the one who'd been keeping him up at night, but maybe he could find a spot on the sand and stare at the stars for a while.

A dozen glass bottles were nestled in an ice-filled tub on a table next to a semicircle of Adirondack chairs. They ringed a stone firepit, facing the water. A couple sat next to a small blaze, talking quietly. He nodded at them, grabbed a beer and wandered to a narrow boardwalk bisecting shore grasses. He walked down the beach a ways and plopped down in the powdery sand.

Not quite the rocky beaches he'd visited on Oyster Island.

He couldn't wait to get back. Matias had declined the partnership proposal, but having a line cook job arranged for the summer gave him time.

He took a shot of the stars with his mobile camera's night mode, opened his messaging app, captioned it "opposite side of the sky from Cassiopeia" and sent it off to Sam.

A chime sounded behind him, and he startled.

Turning, he startled again, and leaned back to try to get a better look. The tall shadow ten feet behind him, backlit by lights from the row of small cabins, was oh so familiar.

"Definitely no Cassiopeia," came the equally familiar, deep voice. "But I think I see the Southern Cross."

"I think *I* see a mirage."

Sam chuckled. "Nope."

"But how…" He blinked once, twice, a dozen times, making sure his eyes weren't failing him. They weren't. His love, the home of his heart, right there, bare toes digging into the sand.

Sam sprawled on an elbow next to Kellan, with his legs stretched in front of him. Broad, beautiful and in Australia instead of Washington state.

"You, Kellan Murphy, look just as good under the southern sky as the northern." Fingers reached up and cupped Kellan's cheek. Lips followed, with a kiss softer than the sand beneath them.

And damn it, they had so much to talk about, so many things unsaid and unexplained and they needed to get through all that. But Sam tasted like toothpaste and a hint of coffee, and on the off chance the things that got said and explained weren't the right things, and they left this beach just as confused and separate as they'd been when they got here, then he was going to enjoy one last kiss.

Chapter Sixteen

Sam dug his fingers into Kellan's hair and plundered his mouth, taking everything offered and more. They sank against the sand, a mess of arms and lips and frustration. The need he'd been trying to suppress clamored in his chest, settling in his belly.

More than physical need. It was soul-deep, twisting his heart in his chest and pushing him to deepen the kiss. Sand stuck to his sweat-damp skin. He ignored it. Yeah, he hated getting sand everywhere. He hated the idea of living life without this man, of this being their last kiss, more.

He couldn't cut it short.

But after a minute, he forced himself to withdraw. Breath sawed from his lungs as he put a few inches of space between them. He kept a hand on Kellan's hip.

Confusion returned to the handsome planes Sam had been dreaming of for days. "You're here."

"Yup. The Whitsundays were on my wall."

"No, they weren't." Kell sat up straighter, legs criss-crossed, and Sam's hand fell to the sand. "I remember the maps. Egypt and the Philippines, somewhere in the Caribbean, Mexico, Florida, I think. And then the broken one was definitely Indonesia."

"And the Whitsundays."

"*Sam.* I... I memorized that wall. I know what was there when I left."

"Been a few days since then." Sam pulled out his cell and scrolled through his pictures. He held it out for Kell to see, knowing it was clear enough. A map of Western Australia hung in the middle of all the others, with a marker over this exact beach.

Kell lifted his chin. "You added it."

"Needed to be official."

He gave Kell a minute to notice the other two changes. A map of the southern coast of Ireland, with a star marking a little village east of Cork.

And a picture of the two of them Archer had snapped when they returned from paddleboarding, both with wild, wet hair and unstoppable grins.

Kell pointed at the screen, at the picture taken off the dock. "That's not a shot from a destination, Sam."

"It was the day I set out on what I'm hoping is going to be the best adventure of all," Sam said, putting the device away. "The day I started to fall in love with you."

"You know the moment?" Kell asked quietly.

"Why do you think I pitched off my paddleboard? The sun was shining, and you looked so determined and I couldn't take my eyes off you. Lost my concentration. Ended up in the drink. And when you slid in and joined me, even though you were scared, it was the end for me. Or, the beginning."

"It was a wave, Sam."

"No, Kellan. It was you."

Sam wove his fingers through Kell's, much like his heart was begging him to do with his life.

"I'm not here because it's the Whitsundays, Kellan." His voice ached, straining around all the words bursting to get out of him, the regret that he'd needed so long to figure out his path. "I'm here for you." Sam's gaze lowered and he swirled a finger in the sand. "And for me."

"Are you, now?"

"Can't get you back if I don't know what I want, separate from you."

"And what is it you want? Separate from me?"

Sam chuckled. "Nothing I don't already have. My shop, the ocean, my apartment, my family. I can't ask for more."

"Why not?"

"Because it's not about wanting something different. Yes, I need to balance things better. But once I figure that out, there would still be something missing. I want my shop, and to be out on the water, and living in my apartment again while still caring for and loving my family. But I want it *with* you." He took a shuddering breath. "Will you come back to Oyster Island? Will you stay?"

Kell paused, looking confused. "I'm already planning to, Sam."

"I know. But I need to ask. For you to know I want you there, and that I'm breaking all the rules I made for myself after Alyssa left. I keep thinking of the middle of January when the power's been out for three days because a tower blew down, and we're eating canned soup heated on a camp grill and our phones are long out of batteries. It's those moments when it's easy to want to leave. I didn't think I could ask someone to share that with me again. Didn't want to risk someone not wanting all the realities of island life. But with you—I close my eyes, and all I picture is mixing my life so thoroughly with yours that I don't know where my things end and your things begin."

"Tinned soup on a camp grill?" Kellan made a face. "You honestly believe I couldn't do better than that during a power outage?"

Sam choked on air. "I say all that, and the part you fixate on is store-bought chicken noodle?"

Kellan squeezed his hand. "If my days are made up of moments where I get to keep you warm and share meals and lie in bed with you listening to the wind howl, it'll be a life well lived, Sam. Dead mobile batteries don't scare me. I fully intend to steal one of your cardigans and spend the cold nights snuggling under that knitted blanket I've been eyeing at the shop next to your mum's bakery. Or those lazy days of summer where I go overboard in your dad's yard and grow enough veg to feed everyone you know. Buying the big bottle of shampoo so we can share. So long as you can believe I'm in it for the long run."

"I will."

"Simple words." Kellan's mouth flicked up. Amusement, maybe? Doubt? "Big intent."

"Yeah." Sam rested his elbows on his knees and tented his hands. "I... I have something else to ask, and I can't decide if it's bigger or smaller than asking you to stay."

"I'm listening..."

"You asked Matias if he'd go into business with you," Sam said. "And he declined."

"His 'no' doesn't end my plans. Promise. Cooking for him for a short time will give me something to do for the summer, time to get settled, time to find my place."

"I was hoping you'd say your place is with me."

"I didn't want to plan on that," Kellan murmured.

"I do."

A bark of laughter echoed across the water. "Yet more simple words with big intent."

Sam met the chuckle with one of his own. "I hadn't planned on going near *I do*. Not yet."

"Neither had I, but now that you say it, it's something I'd want on the table in the future."

"Me, too." He took Kellan's hand, the hand he could absolutely see holding in the years to come. "For now, I have a different proposal for you. Work with me."

"I know you need an employee, Sam, but I don't

see completing the training and hours I'd need to dive—"

"Not diving, sweetheart. Cooking."

"For whom?" Kellan asked, puzzled. "Your mum?"

"No, for me. For us. Let's create something together. We can forage, gather, dive with people during the day. And then in the evening, you can take what we've gathered and turn it into something incredible. Something different every meal, if you like. And once we're done? We go home. Together."

Sam's heart pounded in his chest, like the bow of the boat slamming into the waves during a hurricane-force wind.

"Wow," Kellan said, the exclamation weighty with thought. He stroked his chin and stared out at the water.

"It wouldn't have to be full-time," Sam threw out in desperation. "Just a couple days a week, and you could take over Matias's kitchen for breakfast, or hell, build a sister restaurant to Aisling at Hideaway Wharf. Whatever you like. I just—while you do any and all of that...please be my partner."

"I am your partner, a chroí. My heart." Kellan kissed him, as fierce as the storm in his veins, as soothing as the slap of the waves on the shore. "And if we can find a way to make a living taking people out to hunt for fiddleheads and mushrooms and to serve up sea urchin for them—I think it's brilliant."

"You do?"

"There is nothing I want to do more than build a life with you, Sam. You're the man I love. Working together would be marvelous. But it's the 'going home together' part that matters most."

"Knowing that when I wake up, the first thing I lay eyes on is you," Sam said softly.

"Apologies in advance for my bedhead." Kellan's smile was wide.

Sam pulled him into a hug and they fell to the sand. The weight of this man on his chest would carry him into the future, anchor him when stress had him spinning off the ground.

"Do you still feel scared?" Kellan kissed along the V neckline of Sam's T-shirt.

"I… No. I'm nervous. But more from the anticipation. I've been panicking all week, putting plans in place so I could meet you here and have this conversation. And now we're having it, and my chest is pretty much bursting, but it's because I'm excited. Not afraid."

"If the panic comes back, we'll talk through it."

"We will."

"For this week, though—let's just enjoy it," Kellan said. His hand trailed between Sam's pecs and over his stomach. "And each other."

Sam stilled it with his own hand. "Your room, or mine? Let's not get kicked out of the resort before we have the chance to get started. We have beaches to clean and fish to count."

"Our first of many adventures. And then…" Those eyes held all the promises a man could hope for.

"Then we plan another one?" Sam asked. There

were endless possibilities, endless things he wanted to see and do with Kellan Murphy.

Including just soaking in his smile for the rest of his days.

Smiling lips kissed his, tasting of salt and love. "Then, Sam, I pack up my sorry little life in London, and I finally come home."

Epilogue

On the first day of September, sun still warming the air with late summer rays, Kellan unhooked the wooden Otter Marine Tours sign from its place under the eaves. He laid it on a makeshift work table on the shop's porch. He was tight on time to get the second sign attached and to rehang the pair. He had maybe twenty minutes before Sam drove off the ferry, having spent the night in Seattle sourcing new dive tanks. A convenient errand. Kellan had thought he'd need to invent a reason to get his love off the island so that he could set up the new sign—and a bigger surprise—in peace.

Sam's dad stood next to Kellan's table, eyeing the sign he'd carved into a piece of driftwood. FOREST + BRINE was in beautiful relief, painted in the green gradient of Kellan and Sam's new brand.

"Want me to get these eyebolts in, son?" Greg asked matter-of-factly.

Son. It'd not taken long for Sam's family to welcome him in. He'd spent more hours with Greg over the course of the summer than he had in decades with his own father, so *son* felt apt. He'd gained more than Sam when he'd moved to Oyster Island—he'd gained a father figure who loved and respected him. His heart filled.

"You're the artist," Kellan said. "Probably better if you do it."

They were having a Labor Day grand opening come Monday, but tonight was just for him and Sam.

As he watched Greg screw in the bolts, he ran through his to-do list for the decor in the small studio apartment upstairs from Otter Marine, two doors over from the home he and Sam now shared. He and Greg had transformed the studio into a cooking and eating space, renovated on the days Greg had felt able to work. Some of Forest + Brine's trips would end with beach picnics or barbecues, but not on inclement winter days. When, on meeting with Aoife's lawyer prior to leaving London for the last time, Kellan had discovered there was more money than he'd anticipated. He'd decided to put it into the foraging business Sam had proposed.

But watching Greg hook the two parts of the sign together, his neck tingled with second thoughts.

"What if he doesn't like it?" Kellan said, worry filling his chest. "I shouldn't have kept it a surprise."

"The sign, or the apartment?"

"All of it." He scrubbed his face with his hands and swore.

"Deep breath. You were doing an old man a favor by keeping the project quiet. Do you know how many people would have been up in my business if they'd known I was doing the grunt work?" Greg held up the finished product and Kellan took it, the two chunks of wood weighty in his hands. "I needed the reminder I can create beautiful things despite dealing with pain. And getting to do something for my son was a privilege."

"I'm just amazed we managed to keep it from him."

It'd not been easy to schedule all the deliveries and Greg's work sessions for times when Sam had been out on the water. They'd had to let Franci in on the secret right away, given she'd taken over all the in-store hours and promotional work for the dive shop and had witnessed the construction noise overhead. Archer had gotten in on it, too—he'd spread the story that someone from out of town was renting the space long-term and fixing it up to move in come autumn. That had kept Sam from asking too many questions when he noticed new appliances and furniture arriving.

Yesterday marked Kellan's last day working the line for Matias. It had been a good way to spend the summer, finding his feet on Oyster Island and in the community, but he couldn't wait to see where the fall, winter, and spring would take them now that there was an official space to entertain customers.

"Maybe I should wait until Sam gets home to hang

this." From the sign to the paint color on the walls upstairs to the dark blue enamel range he'd spared no expense in purchasing—what if his surprise was unwelcome? Finding out Sam didn't like it and having to take it down would hurt Greg so much. He'd put as much work into this project as Kellan.

It would hurt you, too.

"You should put it up as planned," Greg said. "Use some of those balloons to draw attention to it." He pointed at his daughter, who approached with decorations she'd put together for Kellan.

Franci's smile matched the cheer of the two balloon clusters in either hand. She plopped the two weighted sprays next to his work table and rested her hands on her gently rounded belly. "Two bouquets. Now we just need one brother, and your party can start."

Okay. Let's do this. Kellan fumbled with the two boards of the joined signs. He stood on the top of the step stool and slotted the eyebolts over the hooks.

The door to the store creaked open and Archer leaned against the jamb with his arms crossed. "Looks good."

"Can we get a tour upstairs before Sam gets here?" Franci asked.

"Ferry's arriving." Archer's gaze flicked from the sign to Kellan, Greg, the remaining mess.

"I want Sam to be the first to see it," Kellan said. His hands were starting to shake. He jammed them in his shorts pockets.

Franci nodded and took her dad's elbow. "We'll

wait inside with Arch and peek through the front window. I want to see his face."

Kellan had just enough time to stash the tools and worktable and set up the balloons on the stairs to the upper floor before the line of ferry traffic started winding around the corner and down Port Street.

A familiar black pickup pulled into one of the angled spots in front of the commercial strip.

Sam bounded out and approached the porch. "A one-man welcome party? You missed me that much?"

"Sure." Truthfully. Until last night, they'd spent every night together since Kellan arrived from London mid-May. Desperate to reconnect after too many hours apart, he collided with Sam. Their mouths tangled together, hot and needy. Sam's baseball cap fell to the ground.

He loved this man. This man loved him. He'd have to know what Kellan had done was meant as a happy surprise, a gift.

After countless seconds, Sam pulled away and retrieved his hat. His eyes were glazed. "Some kiss, sweetheart."

"I figure it's kind of like snogging under the mistletoe."

"Huh?"

Kellan took Sam's hands and looked up at the sign overhead.

Sam's brows knitted as he studied the sign, first in confusion, then in something approaching awe.

"Holy crap, it's perfect! Did you have Dad make it?"

Kellan nodded. "He was thrilled to help."

"Thank you for surprising me. I cannot wait to dive into our first trips this month."

"Literally," Kellan cracked, laughing at the pun.

Sam smiled sheepishly and glanced over Kellan's shoulder at the front of the store. "Oh, wow, everyone came for the sign reveal?"

The door burst open and Franci spilled out, hugging Sam. Archer and Greg followed, and even Charlotte and Nic, who weren't party to the upstairs surprise.

"Isn't it gorgeous?" Franci said.

"Incredible job, Dad," Sam said, clapping his father's shoulder. "Good to see you woodworking again."

Greg shot Kellan a questioning look.

Kellan nodded, feet itching to sprint up the stairs, Sam in tow, and show off their hard work. He was surrounded by people he loved in a way he'd never anticipated but would never take for granted. He owed Aoife so much—her final wishes had blossomed beyond adventure into a new family. And at the center of it was the loving, devoted diver wearing a Seattle Kraken T-shirt and a pound of suspicion on his enchanting face.

"Not the only work I've done around here lately, Sam," Greg said, cheeks a chuffed pink.

Sam scanned the crowd, eyes narrowed. "What have you all been up to?"

"Don't look at me." Charlotte pouted. "I'm as in the dark as you."

"Need-to-know basis, peanut," Greg said. "It was hard enough keeping it from Sam."

Sam stacked his hands on his hat-covered head. "Keeping what from me?"

"Let's show him," Kellan said to Greg.

"Together?" Greg was puzzled. "Thought you wanted to do it alone."

"You deserve to see his reaction as much as I do." He shot Sam's dad a *sure hope he loves it* look. Taking Sam's hand, he squeezed. "Don't be mad."

"Mad at what?"

Kellan tugged Sam toward the stairs, leading his love and their band of merry family members past the balloon decorations and up to the door that hid his folly. "You know how it was important for you to ask me to stay?"

Sam nodded.

"Well, it was important for me to do this." Kellan reached for the doorknob, hand shaking.

Sam laid his fingers over Kellan's. "Sweetheart, are you the mysterious out-of-towner Archer told me about?"

"I thought you'd clue into that description fitting me, but I guess you didn't."

"Because you're not an out-of-towner."

The words lifted him like a wave—a gentle roller, not a thunderous crash. He wasn't startled anymore by being thought of as a local. He was just moved. Healed.

And head over heels for the man currently gripping his hand.

"I wanted you to see I'm all in on Forest + Brine.

I know you worried about that, having come up with the idea."

"Okay…"

"Open the door, son!" Greg said.

"Yeah, hurry up before I give birth on the stairs!" Franci said.

"You're not even at six months, Franci. Don't joke about that," Charlotte scolded. Nic whispered something in her ear and her serious expression softened.

Kellan took a deep breath. "Here goes."

He swung the door open and waved Sam into the airy, open space.

He'd been seeing the details of the renovation in his dreams. Had needed to throw out a few articles of clothing, too, so that Sam wouldn't ask why he was covered in flecks of Gloucester Sage and White Heron.

Knowing every inch of the space meant he could watch Sam take in all the hard work instead.

Wonder lit Sam's eyes. "You made this for Forest + Brine? For us?"

"Your dad and I did."

Sam stepped into the center of the room, slowly treading the refinished hardwood, running his hands along the custom-built table for twelve Greg had crafted, and the slab of pine that served as an island. A sumptuous couch and chairs circled both the water view and the for-show woodstove, perfect for post-dinner drinks.

Everyone else wandered in, exclaiming over how pretty it was and praising Greg's woodworking skills.

"Had to take it slow, but I managed," Greg explained.

Sam, though, was quiet. His eyes were wet. He took off his hat and fidgeted with the brim.

Kellan stroked Sam's face with both hands. "If I screwed up, I'm sorry. We can renovate if you don't like it, or I can just use it for catering or for special event tasting dinners or something—"

"Stop." Sam kissed him softly. "I was just...the timing..."

"Is wrong?"

"Hell, no." He blew out a breath. "Kell, sweetheart..." He glanced at their family, who were all milling around, exclaiming over the shiny range and the stoneware made by a local potter, not paying any mind to Kellan and Sam. "I'm going to assume our family being here for your surprise means you won't kill me for having them here when I do this."

Confusion swirled. "When you—" Sam pulled a jewelry box out of his pocket and Kell gasped. "*Oh.*"

"Why do you think I went to Seattle?"

"For dive tanks!"

Shaking his head, Sam knelt on one knee, holding out the boxed pair of simple bands. Happy gasps erupted as everyone slowly clued in to Sam's proposal.

"I figure you were due some more simple words with big intent," Sam said.

"And I've got one for you, depending on the question."

"There's no question, Kellan!" Franci interjected. "We're keeping you. Full stop."

"How about letting me take care of this so that he doesn't run away from all our chaos?" Sam lifted an eyebrow at his sister, then plucked out one of the rings. "They're engraved on the inside. I can't return them." A rueful grin. "I'm really hoping you say yes."

"This isn't chaos, it's love," Kellan said, straightening his fingers and thrusting his left hand toward his boyfriend. *My fiancé.*

Sam slid the ring on his finger and rose, stealing a kiss on the way to standing. "So, yes, then?"

Kellan took the other ring from the box, smiling as he caught the engraving on the inside. He placed the band on Sam's offered ring finger, punctuated by cheers and clapping from their makeshift audience.

"How could I say anything *but* yes, a mhuirnín," he said, echoing the endearment Sam had chosen to mark his ring for a lifetime. He needed to peek at his own, but he bet it said *sweetheart.* "You're the love I've always wanted. The love I plan to keep."

* * * * *

Look for Franci's story,
A Hideaway Wharf Holiday
the next installment in Love at Hideaway Wharf
USA TODAY *bestselling author Laurel Greer's*
new miniseries for Harlequin Special Edition
On sale October 2023, wherever Harlequin
books and ebooks are sold.

#3001 THE MAVERICK'S SWEETEST CHOICE
Montana Mavericks: Lassoing Love • by Stella Bagwell
Rancher Dale Dalton only planned to buy cupcakes from the local bakery. Yet one look at single mom Kendra Humphrey and it's love at first sight. Or at least lust. Kendra wants more than a footloose playboy for her and her young daughter. But Dale's full-charm offensive may be too tempting and delicious to ignore!

#3002 FAKING A FAIRY TALE
Love, Unveiled • by Teri Wilson
Bridal editor Daphne Ballantyne despises her coworker Jack King. But when a juicy magazine assignment requires going undercover as a blissfully engaged couple, both Daphne and Jack say "I do." If only their intense marriage charade wasn't beginning to feel a lot like love...

#3003 HOME FOR THE CHALLAH DAYS
by Jennifer Wilck
Sarah Abrams is home for Rosh Hashanah...but can't be in the same room as her ex-boyfriend. She broke Aaron Isaacson's heart years ago and he's still deeply hurt. Until targeted acts of vandalism bring the reluctant duo together. And unearth buried—and undeniable—attraction just in time for the holiday.

#3004 A CHARMING DOORSTEP BABY
Charming, Texas • by Heatherly Bell
Dean Hunter's broken childhood still haunts him. So there's no way the retired rodeo star will let his neighbor Maribel Del Toro call social services on a mother who suddenly left her daughter in Maribel's care. They'll *both* care for the baby...and maybe even each other.

#3005 HER OUTBACK RANCHER
The Brands of Montana • by Joanna Sims
Hawk Bowhill's heart is on his family's cattle ranch in Australia. But falling for fiery Montana cowgirl Jessie Brand leads to a bevy of challenges, and geography is the least of them. From two continents to her unexpected pregnancy to her family's vow to keep them apart, will the price of happily-ever-after be too high to pay?

#3006 HIS UNLIKELY HOMECOMING
Small-Town Sweethearts • by Carrie Nichols
Shop owner Libby Taylor isn't fooled by Nick Cabot's tough motorcycle-riding exterior. He helped her daughter find her lost puppy...and melted Libby's guarded emotions in the process. But despite Nick's tender, heroic heart, can she take a chance on love with a man convinced he's unworthy of it?

Get 3 FREE REWARDS!

We'll send you 2 FREE Books plus a FREE Mystery Gift.

FREE
Value Over
$20

Both the **Harlequin® Special Edition** and **Harlequin® Heartwarming™** series feature compelling novels filled with stories of love and strength where the bonds of friendship, family and community unite.

HARLEQUIN
PLUS

Try the best multimedia
subscription service for romance
readers like you!

Read, Watch and Play.

Experience the easiest way to get
the romance content you crave.

Start your **FREE TRIAL** at
<u>www.harlequinplus.com/freetrial</u>.